The Queen's Own Grove

Patricia Beatty

Illustrated by Liz Dauber

Riverside, CA
2012

Riverside Museum Press
Riverside Museum Associates
Riverside, CA

ISBN 0-9671154-5-0

Contents

The Queen's Own Grove

One Farewell to Nightingale Close

ONLY TWO DAYS before the world fell in on us, she said it again at tea. "You are fortunate children, Amelia, Edmund, and Theodora." Grandmother Thorup fixed us with her eyes while we squirmed on the hard chairs she said were so excellent for our growing spines and our posture. "Your father, Mr. Bromfield-Brown, has an excellent position, and you have a certain social standing here in Chiswick. You live in a very nice house in quite a fashionable section of London. It is probable, too, that one of your Thorup aunts—one at least—will leave you a good deal of money when she dies. You should give thanks for all of this."

Grandmother Thorup squeezed some lemon into her tea, nodded her head, and went on. "It could even be that someday before too long the Queen will knight a member of the Bromfield-Brown family!"

This was always the signal for our mother to murmur politely, "Do you really think so, Mother?"

Grandmother Thorup took a Peerless Biscuit and said with a sniff, "That is my studied opinion, Enid. Queen Victoria cannot fail to recognize the worth of the family. It's just a pity that there are no Thorup men about, now that your dear father has passed on to his reward."

At that Edmund pinched me, reaching around behind the back of his chair. He teases me, as brothers do when sisters are ticklish. I'm Amelia, and I'm ticklish, and at tea I couldn't kick Edmund. He always knew when I wanted to giggle at Grandmother Thorup.

The trouble with Grandmother Thorup was that she resembled Queen Victoria. When she was a young girl and the Queen was young, too, somebody had told her that she looked like the Queen. Grandmother had taken it to heart. As Father said, "She has grown old along with the Queen," and sometimes he added under his breath, "and she's loved every minute of it." Grandmother dressed exactly like the Queen, who was a widow now, too. The Queen wore black dresses and white lace caps and so did Grandmother Thorup. Grandmother read everything she could find about the Queen in the newspapers.

Once I told Edmund, who is eleven, and Theodora, who's only nine, what I really thought. "I think Grandmother thinks she is the Queen!"

For a wonder Edmund was pleasant to me and agreed. Most of the time he has no respect for me at all, even if I am two whole years older than he is. "She's copying the Queen."

"Yes," said Theodora. "I hate Grandmother Thorup!"

We didn't even tell Theodora that it was bad to hate people, because we sometimes thought Grandmother Thorup didn't like us, either. After all, we were only half Thorup.

Worse than that, though, when it came to which side of the family we favored we were all Bromfield-Brown. We looked like our father. We were tall and thin and had auburn hair, bluish-green eyes, and a long face. We even had the pointed Bromfield-Brown nose, which Grandmother did not care for. The Thorups were handsome people and of sturdy stock, according to Grandmother. They had been people of substance ever since the last century.

There were no afflictions in the Thorup line. The same could not be said for the Bromfield-Browns. We all had the "Bromfield-Brown chest"—not that it had shown up in us children yet.

But as Grandmother told us every time it rained, and everyone knows it rains constantly in England, "We all know about Roger Bromfield-Brown's history. You must be careful, children!"

We all *did* know. We didn't need Grandmother Thorup to tell us. Our father had been a victim of consumption—tuberculosis—when he was our age. He had spent a long time in bed until the doctor had finally told him he was cured. That was back in 1865. Now it was 1886, and he'd been fine ever since. Nonetheless, Mother worried that he worked too hard in his office in the city where our man, Cook's husband, drove him every day in our carriage.

It was a Saturday afternoon in early September when it happened to us Bromfield-Browns—the world falling in, I mean.

It was another rainy day and we were all three up in the attic of our house on Nightingale Close. We'd wanted to go outside to walk along the Thames and watch the boats and barges that sailed back and forth all day on the river, but Grandmother Thorup had caught us at the door.

"What are you thinking of?" she boomed at us, so loudly that the maids popped their heads out of the rooms they were cleaning and we heard Cook's footsteps as she started to come up from belowstairs. Grandmother spoke in a very loud voice. She was a little deaf, but she wouldn't use the ear trumpet Mother bought for her. "You're not going out in this weather! You'll get your feet wet and catch your death. Up, up, up!" She waved toward the ceiling. "Go up to the nursery—not belowstairs. Leave Cook and the maids alone. We're having supper guests tonight, and they have their work to do."

Sighing, we put the umbrellas back into the umbrella stand and hung up our capes. Then, muttering to ourselves, we went upstairs—not to the nursery we'd outgrown donkey's years past, but to the attic where Grandmother Thorup's old trunks were stored.

She'd been out to India before Grandfather Thorup had died. He was in the army and was stationed in Bombay. Grandmother didn't know that we played with his sword and sun helmet and with her old cloaks and bonnets. She wouldn't have permitted it, of course.

Edmund had some Peerless Biscuits in his pocket. He gave me one and Theodora one and kept three for himself.

"Do you think Queen Victoria really eats Peerless Biscuits, too?" Theodora asked us.

"I hope she does," I told her. Our father and his brothers owned the Peerless Biscuit Company. Peerless Biscuits came in a fine square black tin with gold lettering and the words, *By Appointment to Her Majesty, the Queen,* on it. Those words meant that Bromfield-Brown biscuits were at Windsor Castle and Buckingham Palace and Balmoral in Scotland, and everywhere else Queen Victoria lived.

"What kind of biscuit do you suppose the Queen likes best?" Edmund said to me as he polished off the last one.

"I don't know." I was still angry because we hadn't been able to go down to the Thames. I would rather have given my biscuit to the ducks and the swans there than have eaten it in the gloomy attic. "Whatever kind Grandmother Thorup likes, I suppose."

"Oh, that's—" But Theodora never got to end her sentence, for Edmund said, "Be quiet!" Edmund had very sharp ears, so we hushed and listened.

Saturdays on Nightingale Close were almost as quiet as Sundays were—and there was nothing in all the world as quiet as Sunday in Chiswick, Father had told us once. He'd sighed as he said it.

But now we heard hoofbeats, rapid hoofbeats, almost the clatter of a canter on our street. Edmund, who had been sitting on one of the trunks, jumped up and went to the little round window that looked out on our street. "It's our carriage!" he told us.

But Father never came home from the city until after dark! Not believing our ears, we ran over to join Edmund at the window. I used my handkerchief to clean off the dusty glass, and Theodora flattened her nose against the pane.

We three watched as Cook's husband, a big man in a black coat and top hat, leaped down from the carriage. We saw him open the door, and we gasped as he helped Father down and then up the walk to our front steps. Father wasn't wearing his hat, and even from four stories up we could see the handkerchief he was holding to his mouth.

"Something's wrong!" Theodora wailed, and darted away toward the door and the stairs before we could catch her. Edmund and I ran at her heels, flying down the narrow steps to the hall, our hands barely touching the railing.

But all at once Theodora came to a sudden stop on the bottom step, and I almost fell forward onto Edmund, stopping behind her. We stood stock-still.

Our father was just coming inside. His arm was over Cook's husband's shoulder. We could see red stains on the handkerchief he held.

Mother and Grandmother Thorup were hurrying out of the parlor. Mother had her hand over her heart and a handkerchief to her face, too. "What is it? What is it?" she cried.

Cook's husband answered her, " 'E's gone and 'ad 'isself one of 'em again."

I heard Edmund draw in his breath in a gasp. We knew what Cook's husband meant.

While Mother began to cry, Grandmother Thorup took charge of everything. "Take Mr. Bromfield-Brown to his bedroom," she told Cook's husband. "Then go fetch Dr. Gumm." She turned to us. "Children, get off the staircase."

We didn't need to be told twice. We three stood to one side as the men went up a flight of steps and inside Father and Mother's room. Father kept his head down. He didn't even look at us. Mother brushed past and tried to smile at us even though she was still crying.

"What is it, Amelia?" Theodora whispered. Her eyes were round with fear. "Is it the White Plague?"

"Yes," I told her. "It's come back to Father."

Grandmother Thorup caught my words. She paused for a second before she went into the bedroom, too, and told us, glaring, "It's the curse of the Bromfield-Browns—that weak chest!"

A few minutes later Cook's husband came lumbering out to go for the doctor.

"What'll we do?" Theodora asked me, since I was the oldest. "Do you think we'd better go to the nursery now?"

"No," I told her. "I don't want to. I want to wait until Dr. Gumm gets here."

Edmund sat down on the bottom step. We sat beside him. Big tears ran down the sailor collar of my sister's blue dress. They made wet, black spots. I put my arm around her and although nobody spoke, I knew we were all thinking the same thing. Was Father going to die? His only sister had died from a hemorrhage of the lungs. Grandmother Thorup had told us *all* about her.

After what seemed like a long time Dr. Gumm came. He was an old, fat man with Dundreary whiskers, and he usually wore a brown-and-white checked coat. We didn't like him very much, but he knew a lot about people's chests and things like that. Twice a year he poked and thumped and prodded us, and every time one of us got a cold he came to the house and gave us more thumpings and nasty-tasting medicine.

We moved over on the stairs to make room for

him, and he went right by us as if we weren't there. After a moment Edmund whispered, "Come on."

We tiptoed up the stairs as quietly as we could. There hadn't been much noise from Father's room while we'd been waiting, only the sound of Grandmother's feet going back and forth, but now we could hear voices, Grandmother Thorup's and the doctor's deep growling one.

We didn't even have to put our ears to the door to hear what they were saying. Dr. Gumm was speaking to our mother. "Mrs. Bromfield-Brown, years ago I told your husband and his entire family that his consumption could return someday. He has had a hemorrhage today, fortunately not a serious one. He will recover."

Mother didn't say anything, but we could hear her crying.

The doctor went right on. "There's something I must tell you. I'd hoped that I would never be forced to say it, but now I am."

"What's that?" Grandmother barked at him.

"You must leave London. These fogs and rain will kill Mr. Bromfield-Brown if he stays here."

"But this is our home!" Grandmother almost shouted at him.

"I will not be responsible for his health or for the health of anyone in this family if all of you don't leave London very soon."

"But where shall we go?" Mother asked softly.

"We'll go to Sussex, or perhaps to Cornwall. The air is purer there in the country," said Grandmother Thorup, sounding determined.

"No." Doctor Gumm was firm. He'd never got along with her very well. "You must leave England!"

Grandmother was shocked. "Leave *England?*"

"That is exactly what I said, Amanda Thorup. Pack up and go to Canada. That's where I send patients who are as ill as Mr. Bromfield-Brown."

"But why Canada?" I heard Mother ask.

"I do not wish to send your husband to a rest home here in England. In Canada he can rest in sunshine and fresh air, and if he is wise he'll stay there."

"But that means we'll emigrate," came from Mother. She sounded strange. I knew how she must feel—just the way I did, as if the world had come to an end.

"And that means we'll be *Colonials*," boomed Grandmother Thorup. "Why, there's nothing in Canada but red Indians and wild animals!"

"There's one thing more in Canada, Amanda Thorup," said Dr. Gumm's voice. "There are men there—men still living twenty years after London doctors gave them up for dead. If you don't go, I won't give you a farthing for Mr. Bromfield-Brown's chances."

Edmund and Theodora and I looked at one another. I guessed I must have been as pale as they were. "Canada!" breathed Theodora, just as if she'd never heard of the place. I knew she had, though. All three of us had been studying about the Queen's Empire at our school, St. Oswald's. We'd got through Australia and Canada and would start learning about India Monday.

Dr. Gumm didn't speak for a little while. Then he told Mother, "Give your husband two teaspoons of this medicine every half hour, Mrs. Bromfield-Brown. He must remain in bed now. I'll leave two prescriptions for him to be filled at the chemist's. If there's any change in his condition, send your man to my house at once."

I heard Mother say, "Thank you." Then came the clumping of the doctor's heavy boots.

What if we were caught eavesdropping? The three of us got back into the shadows of the landings as best we could.

But we didn't have to worry. Dr. Gumm and Grandmother Thorup swept right past without even seeing us. They stopped in the hall below and we came to the banisters and peeked through.

"Now, sir, is it *really* necessary for us to leave England?" Grandmother Thorup asked him.

"Madam, I don't care a fig for what *you* do or

where *you* go! But my patient must be on his way by the tenth of October if he is to live."

"That soon?"

"Yes. Crossing the Atlantic in early autumn will be much easier for him."

"Oh, dear." For the first time we heard Grand-mother Thorup almost whimper. "And I was so very seasick when Mr. Thorup and I went out to India."

"I am sure you will survive. Keep the children away from Mr. Bromfield-Brown for their safety." The doctor tipped his hat to her and went out the door that one of the frightened maids held open for him.

When she came back upstairs Grandmother caught us trying to sneak up to the nursery. "Aha! Eavesdropping!" she shouted at us. "How common of you. For that you will have no tea today!" With a loud rustle of black taffeta skirts she disappeared into Father's room. We hadn't even had one glimpse inside.

Slowly we climbed the stairs toward the attic. Edmund spoke to me. "Canada's a long way off, isn't it, Amelia?"

"Hundreds and hundreds of miles," I told him, feeling as gloomy as the day outside.

"All the way across the Atlantic Ocean," Theodora added.

Because I was the oldest and because I ought to, I tried to cheer them up. "It'll be different," I told them. "It'll be interesting—I think."

"I wonder if we'll see any red Indians," Theodora wanted to know.

"Course we will. They're all over the place. And they told me in my form at St. Oswald's that they don't scalp people anymore." Edmund looked a little happier. He liked adventures. Boys do. "I think I might get to like it there. Wonder where we'll go, Amelia."

I shook my head. I knew Canada was very, very large. I was more than a little bit afraid of what was going to happen to all of us Bromfield-Browns. I wished we could talk with Father, but the doctor had said we couldn't. I knew what that meant—we might catch tuberculosis, too.

Two   Our Travels

THE NEXT DAY all four of our Bromfield-Brown uncles came to our house. They did not come to tea, so they left their wives and our twelve cousins at home.

They trooped abovestairs and stayed for a little while with Father first, and then they filed into the parlor with Grandmother Thorup and our mother. We children waited on the stairs once more. We wanted to listen, but we were afraid that we'd get caught and have to go hungry in the afternoon again.

After a very long time they all came out, and we heard our oldest Bromfield-Brown uncle telling

Mother, "It's arranged then, Enid. We shall buy Roger out of the company, and I will buy this house, if you think the price I've offered is fair."

"Thank you," Mother told him.

I thought she looked very small standing there, surrounded by our tall uncles in their black frock coats. Everyone told us how pretty our mother was. We liked to look at her when she was dressed up for guests or going out. Today she was wearing her ashes-of-roses silk gown with the bustle and black velvet buttons. I didn't like that dress much, even if it was the latest mode. The color made me think of the old petals in the potpourri bottle on Grand-mother Thorup's dresser. I liked to see Mother wear brighter colors, but she didn't very often.

Our next-to-oldest uncle had a scratchy high voice. "Don't fret. There will be money for anything reasonable Roger chooses to do in Canada—if he gets his health back." I didn't like this uncle, and I felt my cheeks getting hot when he talked about Father's health that cruel way.

The shortest uncle, our favorite, offered his hand-kerchief to Mother. He was embarrassed, I thought, and offered it to her because he thought she was going to cry and he didn't know what else to do. "I'll get the steamship tickets for you and see that the servants have new places, Enid."

"Thank you, Cyril," Mother murmured. She liked Uncle Cyril, too.

Our fourth Bromfield-Brown uncle, the youngest, was always in a hurry. Father told us once that he was the most ambitious of them all and wanted to make a lot of money, and Grandmother said that he'd probably be the one to be knighted. He took his hat and walking stick from the maid. "Call on us if you need us again, Enid. Just call on us at any time." He bowed briskly to Grandmother and Mother and was out the door.

The others followed him, more slowly and sadly, I thought.

Mother turned away now. She tried to smile. "It does look as if we are on our way to Canada, doesn't it, Mother?"

Grandmother must have been doing some deep thinking about Canada. "Canada is part of the British Empire, Enid. We must never lose sight of that fact. The Colonies are England's children. We must bear that in mind constantly—that we shall really never leave English soil!"

Edmund whispered to me, "Do you think the red Indians in Canada know that, Amelia?"

Our uncles put us and fourteen trunks on the train for Liverpool early in the morning of the sixth of October. We looked gloomily out of the windows of the compartment we shared with Grandmother Thorup, as we left gray, smoky London and went into the west country.

The fields were brown, the hay harvest past, and the windows streamed cold, dirty rain. We didn't find our last sight of England a happy one at all. Liverpool was a small, grimy city, and the Mersey a dull, oily-looking gray river.

Our ship, the *Canberra Princess,* was the same dirty gray. Grandmother and Theodora and I shared a cabin filled with heavy, dark brown furniture, bolted to the deck so it couldn't slide away. Our three bunks were hard and narrow.

We sailed at dawn, and the Irish Sea was filled with fog. Though I strained my eyes we never saw Ireland. In the fog we didn't know when we steamed past Land's End, the last point in England. So Theodora and I, who had decided we'd really have a good cry then, couldn't even cry at the right moment. We supposed we might have asked one of the ship's officers, but they were all so busy and so frightening-looking that we were afraid to bother them.

That first night out we began to learn what an Atlantic crossing could be like. We were too scared to be seasick, at first. The bow of the *Canberra Princess* rose high up and then went down, slapping into the ocean hard and making me think the ship would break in two and we'd all be drowned. It was so rough that we fell all over one another and had to walk bent over in order to get to the dining salon. Our food bounced on the table; we just grabbed at the plates as they skidded by. The sea spray lashed the portholes so hard that we never did get to open them.

Edmund and I went out on deck just once and looked at the gray-green, whitecapped sea heaving and chomping about us. Then Grandmother missed us and sent a steward after us. We thought she was more worried about our Bromfield-Brown chests than about our being washed overboard. The sea was so fearful-looking, though, that we didn't really mind going back inside.

Our father was all right. Mother never left him, and the ship's doctor was there a lot of the time, too. We weren't allowed to see Father except for a half hour a day, and I read to him most of that time. The medicine he took made him very drowsy, Mother told us. We knew he needed to rest.

By the time we had reached the halfway mark we were very bored. We knew that there were other children aboard the *Canberra Princess*, for we caught sight of them in the second-class dining salon when we passed it. But our Bromfield-Brown uncle had bought us first-class tickets. We wished he hadn't. We wanted to have someone to play with, but the ship's rules kept us away from the other children, even if we could have outwitted Grandmother Thorup and got to them.

"Those children are emigrants," said Grandmother Thorup, as she snatched Theodora away from peeking into the second-class lounge again.

"So are we!" came from my sister, and Grandmother glared at her.

I knew there were even more children aboard. They were down in the steerage, down in the bottom of the *Canberra Princess*. We never saw hide nor hair of them. Grandmother had only spoken of them once. The steerage children weren't even from the British Empire, she told us. They were Swedes and Poles and Germans and what-have-you, not the right kind of emigrants for the Empire. She sniffed and began to knit a pair of wristlets for Edmund while he looked sour.

After a long week we landed in New Brunswick at a strange little village called Saint John. We went through customs and had our trunks checked, although I can't imagine what they were looking for. We hadn't taken anything with us that could interest anybody. Grandmother Thorup dealt with the customs men while Mother looked after Father in a wheelchair and we peered out the windows of the cold customs shed.

"Br-r-r," said Theodora, frowning as she looked

up the glass at the icicles that hung down three feet from the eaves.

Saint John was a grim place in the sleety rain. The wooden houses were built on stilts to avoid the frost, and steps led up to them. Ice-filled mud puddles were everywhere around the railroad station and the waiting train. I didn't think Saint John was very nice, even though its people were. They were quite kind to us and gave us candy and talked to us in their odd flat voices.

"Is that the way Canadians talk?" my sister whispered to Grandmother.

"Yes, it seems so," she told Theodora. "We must bear with it. In time we may even become accustomed to it." She sighed.

We got on the train and by late afternoon were on our way. Now it snowed. We'd seen snow in London, but it wasn't the same as snow in Canada. It snowed in Canada all day and all night. It snowed when we arrived in Montreal, where we caught another train for Kingston, Ontario, the place Dr. Gumm had recommended.

It had stopped snowing when we reached Kingston, but the snow there was four feet deep. We looked out of our hotel windows and what a wonderful sight we saw—a man driving a sleigh and a team of blacks across the ice of the Lake Ontario bay, south of Kingston.

"Look!" we called, and Grandmother came—when it was Mother we wanted.

Grandmother Thorup shuddered. "What a dreadful thing to do! The horses will all be drowned. That man hasn't a particle of good sense. You children must never go out on that ice, do you hear me? When we're settled here, we'll find you a tutor so you'll never have to leave the house and expose yourselves to this ghastly cold." She had on three merino shawls and was shivering.

We didn't dare open the window and poke our heads out, or scoop up some of the snow on the ledge to eat, because Grandmother hardly let us out of her sight. Theodora and I gave up. We came away from the window and I listened to my sister read. But Edmund stood at that window most of the day watching the boys below on Prince's Street go by with their sleds and ice skates. He came back with tears in his eyes once and said that the snow dazzled him and made his eyes hurt, but I didn't believe that.

As it turned out, we never went out in the snow at all.

The day after we came to Kingston, Father began to cough heavily again. The doctor, who had been a student of Dr. Gumm's in London, came and examined him. This Canadian doctor was a tall, very broad man with red cheeks. When he entered the room, a breath of wonderful cold fresh air came in ahead of him. We sniffed it and sniffed it until it went away, but Grandmother just pulled her shawls closer over her shoulders.

The doctor called Mother out into our room to talk. "Mrs. Brown," he said, and we all were startled to hear our name said like that. "I don't like to tell you folks this when you've come so far and have just got here, but you'd be wise in my estimation to leave Kingston now."

Grandmother exploded at him. "Good heavens! We haven't been here twenty-four hours. Where do you propose we go—back to England?"

"No," said the doctor calmly. "Go to British Columbia. It has the mildest climate in Canada. It would be better for your whole family," and here he looked at Edmund, Theodora, and me. "These children should not be kept indoors constantly—certainly not with consumption in the home. We are in for a very severe winter in Ontario. I've already sent three of my patients to British Columbia this month, before they and their families are snowbound here for days."

Mother looked at the three of us. "We'll go," she said quietly.

And so we did.

We spent eight days on the train crossing Canada, changing trains once in Toronto.

Father stayed in his berth in another compart- ment, resting while we three watched Canada go by. We saw the eastern forests, the snow-covered trees, and then the plains that went on for hundreds of miles without end. For one whole glorious day we looked at the Rocky Mountains. Even Grand- mother Thorup was impressed by them, although she said that the Himalayas were higher.

"They're both in the British Empire, Grand- mother," Edmund told her, laughing, and he made her so angry that she dropped a stitch in her knit- ting.

Finally we got to Vancouver, and Father left the train on a litter. He grinned at us, though, and waved his hand.

Mother rented a house for us in Vancouver and we went to another school, St. Swithin's, this time. Father spent a few weeks in the hospital and then came home to live with us, so things were a little like Chiswick—except that Father was home all the time and our only servant was a little maid who didn't even live with us.

Vancouver wasn't too different from London when you overlooked the Canadian accents, we kept telling ourselves. It rained a lot there, almost as much as it had rained in England. It comforted Theodora to look up at the mountain formation that looked so much like the British lion that this was what people called it. I thought that the food was better in Vancouver than in England, but I didn't dare say so.

Sometimes when I heard the rain and closed my eyes in my bed at night I could almost believe we were all back home in our house on Nightingale Close. I did a lot of dreaming about London. But our house and Cook and Cook's husband and the maids were gone when I woke up in the morning back in Vancouver.

Edmund and Theodora and I stayed close together at school and after school. We didn't seem to make any friends. We were different. That's what we thought it was, anyhow. Our clothing was different, but the most different thing of all was the way we spoke. The Canadians didn't laugh at us. There were many English, Irish, and Scots in Vancouver, and everyone had heard other accents, but Canadians didn't seem to take to us too much. And there were other troubles, too. We could never ask anyone to come home with us to play because of Father's illness and because of Grandmother Thorup.

Grandmother had decided that she didn't care for Canadians even if Canada *was* part of the Empire.

The few Canadians we got to know in Vancouver didn't care much for Grandmother, either. She fought with the greengrocer and the butcher and with Father's doctor, though Father was improving each day.

She got very angry with the doctor when he let Father and Mother take a trip to Victoria for two days to see about buying into a business there. The doctor was a young man, young enough to be Grandmother's son, and she thought he didn't know his business very well. "It is much too soon for Mr. Bromfield-Brown to be up and gadding about," she told the doctor.

Father took a hand now in the problem with Grandmother. We knew that he was much better when he started doing that. It meant that he had more strength, for it took strength to stand up to her. "Nonsense. I'm going to Victoria!" Father said.

But when he came home from Victoria and had another hemorrhage the next day, Grandmother Thorup had words with the doctor. "See now!" she told him in our parlor while he put his stethoscope away. "Mr. Bromfield-Brown never should have gone to Victoria. You were wrong. I told you so!"

"Mrs. Thorup, I have something to tell *you!*" The young doctor spoke more sternly than we'd ever heard him speak. "Mr. Brown has had a serious setback. Even though it will soon be summer here in British Columbia, he must leave. A hot, dry climate is the only place for him now. He can't have more hemorrhages!"

Grandmother Thorup plunked herself down beside a table. She drummed on it with her fingers, looking as dark as the cloudy February sky outside. "And where do you suggest we go this time, my lad?" she asked.

We three children lined the wall, breathlessly waiting for his answer.

"Maybe we're going to go to Egypt," Edmund said softly to me. "I like the pyramids."

The doctor wasn't afraid of Grandmother. He told her, "California, to be specific. And to be more specific, the southern part of California. The closer Mr. Brown gets to Mexico, the better."

"What an idea! California is not part of the British Empire at all, young man."

"That is correct, Mrs. Thorup. It is part of the United States. And the last time I was in the States, which was about a year ago, I recall that the Americans spoke the English language rather adequately." He nodded to us and picked up his bag. "They might even surprise you by understanding *your* English, madam."

Now he winked at Theodora, not caring a bit if

Grandmother saw him or not. "Good day," he told us all cheerily, "I'll be back this evening to see Mr. Brown."

I don't know where my sister got the courage, but she piped up, "We'll let you in—if Grandmother won't!"

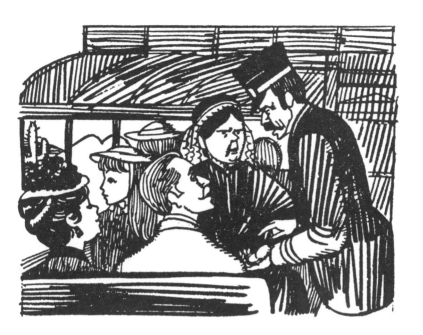

Three   The End of the World

THAT EVENING THE Canadian doctor came again, and this time he talked with Mother and Father. We weren't permitted in Father's room, of course, so we waited in the parlor of the Vancouver house. Grandmother stayed with us. We didn't know whether it was to keep us from eavesdropping or because she was angry with the doctor.

Mother came out to us after he'd gone away. I hadn't seen her look so unhappy since we left London. She didn't speak to Grandmother first this time; she spoke to us. "We are leaving for the United States, children, just as soon as your father can travel."

"We know, Mother," came from Theodora.

Mother sat down on the sofa alone. She didn't put her arm around Theodora, the youngest, the way she usually did when she wasn't happy. After a minute she sighed. "The doctor says we should go to the southern part of the state of California."

We kept quiet, waiting. Then she seemed to brighten a little. "He says that there are quite a few English colonies there."

Now Grandmother Thorup inclined her head a little. "Yes, Enid—now that you mention it, I have heard something of the kind. Wasn't one of the Bromfield-Brown brothers involved in a company in London that sent colonists to the United States? I believe I heard him—Augustus, wasn't it?—say once that the Bromfield-Browns were going to be instrumental in civilizing America."

"Yes," our mother told her. "It was Augustus, the oldest brother."

"Any place an English company sends Englishmen can't be all bad." Grandmother looked a bit brighter, too. She reached for her knitting needles and yarn and began to cast on stitches so swiftly that it made my head ache to watch her. "Where did that silly creature of a doctor suggest we go, Enid?"

"Ontario," Mother told her.

"That's in Canada. We've already been there." Edmund sounded disgusted.

"There's an Ontario in California, too, it seems," Mother explained.

"Well," boomed Grandmother. Then she shivered. "I certainly don't fancy going there, wherever it is." She put down her knitting and nodded her head toward the bookcase. "Amelia, please fetch us the atlas. There must be more suitable places. I saw enough chilly weather in Ontario, Canada, in one day to last me all of my life."

I took down the heavy atlas and put it on the table next to her. It was all I could do to lift it. We'd bought it in Vancouver, and I hoped we wouldn't take it to California with us.

"Find me a map of that state—the one with the odd name," she ordered me.

I found it right off, not telling her the three of us had already looked at California and had talked about its strange jagged shape. On the map of the United States it was green. I had wondered about that. Did that mean the state was a green one, with forests?

Grandmother looked over the top of her spectacles and ran her finger along the map. "Mm-m," she muttered. "What a lot of very queer-sounding names—San Diego, Santa Barbara, Los Angeles.

Well, with names like that, they certainly aren't English places! I wonder whatever they could be?" Her finger moved east. "They have counties in the United States, too, it seems. I wouldn't have thought it of them. That's a great deal like England, to have counties, isn't it? Here's a good-sized county, but the name is foreign, too—San Bernardino. There now, I've found your Ontario, Enid." She muttered to herself a little more and then we heard her sound pleased. Grandmother rarely sounded contented, but when she did she wheezed. She was wheezing now. "Do come here, Enid," she called to Mother. "I've found the English colonies!"

We all crowded around the table and looked at the spot where Grandmother's finger rested. "See here," she said. "I've found a Sunnymead and a Riverside."

"Oh, yes," Theodora breathed beside me, "it's just like going to Windsor Castle from London. I remember the railway stations along the way. There is a Sunnymead and a Riverside."

"This settles it. We go there, then," Mother said, smiling at Grandmother, who was still looking pleased with herself and wheezing slightly.

"Where?" Edmund asked. "Which one?"

Mother looked blank for a moment. "Well, I don't really know. They're both pretty names, and each one or both of them could be something like England."

I spoke up, though I knew I was being overbold. "I like Riverside," I said. "That means there'll be a river, and I miss the Thames."

"So do I, Amelia," Mother said softly to me. "Well, then, we'll go to Riverside instead of Sunnymead."

"Yes, if we must leave the Empire, we shall make the best of it by living among the most civilized people we can find—our own English folk. Riverside sounds as if it has possibilities—distinct possibilities!" Grandmother, as usual, had had the last word.

Mother spoke to the doctor about Riverside, and she wrote Uncle Augustus Bromfield-Brown. The doctor said that Riverside's climate would do admirably for Father, and Uncle Augustus wrote us that there were indeed Canadians and English in Riverside. We weren't interested in the Canadians, but Grandmother was very gratified to learn she'd been right about there being Englishmen in California.

Toward the end of May, the week before we were to leave, the doctor gave us a letter that said Father's tuberculosis was no longer contagious. Now

there was nothing to hold us back from leaving—
nothing except our own fears, and Grandmother
didn't give in to any.

"I consider Vancouver barely part of the Empire,"
she told us. "It is filled with Scots and Irish and
other people who aren't English. We shall try our
luck elsewhere."

Edmund had a thought then. "Do you suppose
there are Americans in Riverside?" he asked her.

"If there are it doesn't matter, Edmund. In an
English community they will have learned how to
keep their place."

We were to go by boat. The trip would be easier
for Father, the doctor told us. And so on a rainy
morning we left Canada behind and went aboard
the *Queen of the Orient*, a ship only half the size of
the *Canberra Princess*. By now I had begun to wonder if all ships were named after monarchs.

Theodora and I cried a little this time as we had
our last look at Vancouver's rock lion. "Are we going
to be Americans?" she asked me.

"I think so," I said. My teacher in Vancouver had
told me that our father would have to become an
American citizen if we were to live in the United
States, but I hadn't told my sister that yet. The idea
upset me. I didn't think I liked Queen Victoria terribly well, but I wasn't too sure that I was going to

like anyone named Grover Cleveland either, even if his last name did sound English. I knew he was the President of where we were going.

Grandmother Thorup came to stand at the rail with us as the mists of the straits drifted over Vancouver, blotting out the city. She drew a deep wheeze of satisfaction. "That's that!" she said loudly. I guessed she was thinking that she wouldn't have to fight with the Vancouver tradesmen anymore and was pleased. Then, her back straight as one of the Coldstream Guards, she went below-decks.

Edmund looked after her. "I wonder if the United States will take to Grandmother Thorup."

Theodora giggled. "Canada didn't!"

It took us a week to sail from Vancouver to San Francisco. The captain let us onto his bridge and inside his chartroom because we were the only passengers he had that trip. Mostly he carried lumber from Canada to the United States, he told us. He put in at Seattle, but we didn't go ashore. It looked a lot like Vancouver to us.

When we docked at San Francisco, even Grandmother was impressed. Its greenish hills were covered with fine buildings of all colors, and the bay in the sunshine was a bright blue with little white skipping waves.

And there in that pretty setting Grandmother had a frightful row with the American customs agent. I don't think I'll ever forget her telling him, "No, young man, I am not attempting to smuggle the crown jewels of England into the United States of America without paying duty on them." While I blushed she stood there fuming as he went through our trunks and valises. When he got to the ninth trunk she told him, "Have a care, young man—that has the carving set inside. You may cut yourself badly." She smiled at him.

He scowled back. Then he marked our trunks *Cleared*, and got away as fast as he could. I don't think he would have cared if the other trunks had had the crown jewels in them. He'd had enough of Grandmother.

"A most disagreeable young person!" Grandmother said to me loudly.

"Ain't that the truth though, lady?" said the man who was waiting to take our trunks to the train station. "Them custom men thinks they got the world by the tail, ma'am. Some of 'em'd go out hunting bear with a switch." He heaved a trunk high up onto his wagon, leaving Grandmother speechless for a full minute.

"What language!" she told me when he was out of earshot. "What ignorance! Did you ever hear such grammar—calling me *lady?* These Americans have much to learn."

"You teach them, Grandmother," Edmund said slyly, but she only nodded.

"He called you *ma'am,*" Theodora said. "That's what people call the Queen. Does that mean he thinks you're Queen Victoria, too?"

Grandmother smoothed out her gloves with a shudder. "I greatly doubt, Theodora, if that person is aware that there is a Queen of England."

We went right to the train station then, for the doctor in Vancouver had warned us about the changeable winds that might be bad for Father's chest.

"We've got to go farther south." Theodora sighed, looking at San Francisco's bright sunshine, and I sighed, too, while the cool breezes whipped my hair from under my hat.

I stood right behind Grandmother when she bought our train tickets, hoping that she wouldn't quarrel again, and luckily she did not. We got tickets on the Southern Pacific. It would take us almost to Riverside with only one other train change, to the California Southern, in Los Angeles.

It took us a day and a half to travel to Los Angeles, four hundred and fifty American miles from San Francisco. We kept our faces glued to the train windows as we went past green meadows, marshes, patches of deep blue Pacific Ocean, and sand dunes. I went on telling myself that it wasn't too very different from parts of England and Canada I'd seen before.

But Los Angeles was a shock! It wasn't a real city at all, not to our way of thinking. It had only a few streets and not many houses. None of them looked much like our tall brick house in Chiswick. Some were big, but they were made of wood or of a queer brownish stuff I'd never seen before.

"Dear me," Mother said as we left the train. "It isn't much of a place, is it?"

Grandmother wasn't dismayed, though. "Now this is not Riverside, Enid. This is one of those foreign places on the map."

"Yes, Mother," said our mother.

We boarded another train that same morning, and now we traveled east, sixty miles inland to Riverside.

All of us, even Father, looked anxiously out the windows as our little train bounced along the rails—rails so new that they had no rust and glittered in the sun.

"I've never seen such sunshine," Father said.

"It makes my eyes ache," added Mother, "and I'm so hot."

That was true. It had been hot in Los Angeles, and on the train it got hotter and hotter.

For once Grandmother didn't have anything to say, but she chewed her lips as we passed by mile after mile of brownish-yellow ground. Now and then we saw a dusty-looking tree and a dusty-looking house, and beyond that what Father said must be a vineyard because it resembled vineyards he'd seen in France. But if it was a vineyard, we didn't see any grapes on the stumpy green bushes. I was confused. I thought grapes grew up in the air on arbors, the way they did in England.

The conductor, a little man in a black suit with a face as brown and wrinkled as a walnut, came along to us and took out his watch. "Next stop's Colton, folks. It'll be in five minutes."

"But where is Riverside?" Grandmother asked him.

"Southeast of here, lady. You have to take a wagon or stage to there from Colton. Train doesn't go that far just yet. Maybe next year, though."

"We haven't seen the river," Father told him.

The conductor spat tobacco juice into a brass cuspidor. "Nope, we don't go over the Santa Ana River. You'll see it in Riverside—if you hurry up."

"If we hurry up?" Mother said, puzzled.

"Yep. Just about gone right now, or at least it

oughter be. It was goin' fast when I looked at it a couple of weeks ago."

"What happened to it?"

"Dryin' up. Happens some summers." He winked at me. "Between the two of us, little lady, it ain't much of a river, 'cept when it goes on a rampage and floods!"

"Then why is where we're going called Riverside?" asked my sister.

"Search me, honey." He laughed. "But sure as shootin', whatever reason there is, it shouldn't be because of the Santa Ana River."

"What do you people in this part of the country do for water?" asked Father. He looked very concerned.

"Oh, it ain't as bad as all that, mister. We got real fine water, even if it is a little bit hard. We got wells, deep ones, and lotsa canals around Riverside."

"Canals like Holland's?" Mother wanted to know.

"Yep, lady. You'd be foreign, wouldn't you? I can tell by the way you talk. Well, there's folks in Riverside who rides this train that tells me there's canals in Holland too. I never been there. They couldn't get along without 'em where you're bound. The canals keep Riverside goin'."

A tall, prickly-looking bush of some sort passed out of my sight as the train clattered along. "What's that strange-looking plant?" I asked.

"That there's a cactus. They grow real good here without needin' water at all. The oranges need water, though. That's what's puttin' Riverside on the map—oranges!"

"Oranges?" Father asked with interest. He liked plants.

"Yep, oranges and lemons and raisin grapes. That's what folks raise in these parts. The only things that grow natural here in this part of the States is cactus, horned toads, and rattlers. They do real good, rattlers do!"

"Rattlers—what are they?" Theodora wanted to know.

"Snakes, missy. Rattlesnakes. They're mean customers, let me tell you."

"Merciful heaven!" Grandmother was very impressed. She was gloomy, too. When the conductor moved on, she looked out the window. The flat, parched-looking ground, dotted with cactus plants, stretched out beyond some wooden buildings to low, yellowish hills. The hills were ringed by blue-violet mountains, under a cloudless sky. The train began to slow down.

Mother tried to cheer Father up, but he didn't look very cheerful.

"No river!" Theodora mourned beside me as we heard the brakes of the train squealing.

"Well!" Grandmother finally snapped out so

loudly that half of the railroad car turned around to look at us, "I seem to have been deceived. I think, Enid, that we have been sold a bill of goods in Vancouver." She waved her hand at the brown country baking in the sun outside. "If this is where we are to live, I have only one thing to say. I have seen India, so I feel that I may say it. Riverside is going to be the absolute end of the world!"

Four   Our Own Grove

WE GOT OFF and stood on the platform at Colton
while our trunks were hauled out of the baggage car
and tumbled onto the platform. Without saying a
word to anyone, I went over and sat down on one of
them. Theodora came with me, gasping for breath,
too.

"It's worse than Cook's oven being open for the
Christmas baking," she said. My sister's face was
getting redder by the minute. So was Edmund's.
He'd unbuttoned his collar and pulled off his hat to
fan his face. Grandmother Thorup even took off her
shawl and put it over her arm. She stood frowning,
looking around at Colton. I guessed how she felt.

Father was talking to a little man who had stomped up onto the platform, leaving his tallyho on the opposite side of the road next to a sign that read, *Marcus Finch, Livery Stable, Horses, Rigs, Wagons for Hire.*

We went on gasping like fish in the heat, which was so dry it made your nose prickle. Some of the passengers who'd been on the train with us drove off in carriages with friends who'd come to meet them. Other passengers walked over toward the livery stable. I noticed that no one walked very briskly. The ladies put up their parasols and the men took off their coats. Watching them, Edmund took off his coat, too.

Grandmother Thorup didn't even seem to notice what he'd done. She was mopping at her face with her handkerchief and her lips kept moving. I could hear her. She said, "It's every bit as bad as I remember. It's every bit as bad as India!"

"No wonder Grandmother left India," my brother muttered. For a minute I thought he was going to take off his shirt, too, but thank heaven, he didn't.

Mother came up to us now. Her nose was shinier than her face and there were little streaks through her rice powder. "We're going to the Rowell Hotel in the tallyho," she told us. "The coachman says there'll be a breeze when we leave here."

Grandmother gazed at the tallyho, a wagon with a cloth shade top, and at the little man, with the pink-and-white striped shirt and red sleeve garters, who stood behind Father, grinning.

"Humph," she snorted loudly, "the tallyho hasn't room in it for us and our baggage, too, Enid."

"I'll come back and get the bags, lady," the little man called out.

"Not on your life, my man," came from Grandmother. "Someone will surely steal our trunks. I learned long ago never to put my trust in the natives. I shall see to it that our things arrive safely."

"But, Mother, how will you do that?" our mother asked her.

Grandmother pointed toward the livery stable. One of the passengers was putting a crate and a trunk into a wagon he'd just hired. "We shall hire a wagon."

"Roger isn't to exert himself, Mother!"

"Who said Roger was going to drive? I'll drive, Enid. You and Roger and the girls can go in the tallyho. Edmund will come with me. It will be an educational experience for him."

"But Mother, you haven't driven for years, and you don't know the way!"

"I was once an excellent driver. Your own father taught me, and no one could drive a team as he could, I'll have you know. As for knowing the way, that will not be necessary. I shall simply follow you in the tallyho to whatever the odd name of that hotel is." She looked sharply at the three of us.

Mother looked disturbed, but gave in. For a minute I thought she wasn't going to. Mother had been growing more and more exasperated ever since we left Los Angeles. "All right," she said, "but do be careful."

Grandmother didn't reply. She motioned to Edmund to come along with her and they started across the street, little puffs of yellow dust coming out on each side of Grandmother's black skirts.

We got up into the tallyho and sat down. Just as we saw Grandmother and Edmund disappear inside the livery stable, our driver clucked to his pair of bays and we were off on the road to Riverside. "Oh, I do hope Mother and Edmund will be all right," Mother said. She was crumpling up her handkerchief and kept looking behind her as some whitish hills blocked Colton from our view.

We heard the hoot of the train whistle after we'd been on our way for about ten minutes. Then a few minutes after that, we heard something else—the sound of wheels coming fast along the dusty road.

Theodora, Mother, Father, and I twisted around to look.

Around the bend of the road came a wagon with two galloping black horses hitched to it. We could see our baggage bouncing in the back. Edmund sat on the seat, hanging on with both hands, while Grandmother Thorup sawed on the reins.

"Darn Finch. He went and done it again!" yelled our tallyho driver as he pulled his bays over to the side to let Grandmother's wild-eyed blacks go by.

"Mother, stop! Stop!" our mother screamed as Grandmother Thorup thundered past.

Grandmother didn't even look back at us. She was too busy calling out, "Whoa, whoa, I tell you!" to the horses. They didn't pay a bit of attention to her, though.

"Edmund, Edmund! My darling!" Mother screamed. She pounded on our driver's back. "Catch them, oh, catch them! That's my little boy there."

"Can't, lady," the tallyho driver told us quite calmly. "Nothin' in San Bernardino County can catch up with Finch's blacks when they hear the train whistle. Finch oughtn't to have hired 'em out to no woman, though. Darn Finch. He'll kill somebody someday." He spat tobacco juice over the wheel. "Well, maybe on second thought, I shouldn't be so hard on old Finch. Maybe the blacks was all he had left to rent out. Lotsa folks on today's train. Yessir, California—leastwise this part of it—is sure boomin' these days. They're callin' it the boom of '87 already."

"But my son and my mother-in-law could be killed," Father protested, cutting off the driver's speech. "Can't you catch up with them?"

The tallyho man from the Rowell Hotel shook his head. "It'd be no use, I tell you. Don't you worry. Your boy was hangin' on good and the old lady wasn't doin' no real yellin'. That's a good sign. Them blacks won't go no farther'n Riverside. Somebody'll stop 'em there. That's only a couple miles ahead. Just the same, I'll hurry up for you." He touched the team with his whip and they broke into a canter.

We passed other rigs and wagons now, our driver tipping his hat politely to each one we passed. "Finch's blacks go this way?" he called out to one driver.

"Sure did," the man yelled back. "Goin' like bats outa hell. That old lady sure's some jockey, ain't she?" He sounded as if he admired Grandmother.

"How was she doing?" our driver called.

"Doin' fine. In a heck of a hurry, though."

There wasn't time to ask anything more, we were going so swiftly ourselves. Mother hung onto the side of the tallyho, a look of fright on her face.

I touched her shoulder. "They're all right,

Mother. Nothing could happen to Grandmother Thorup. You heard what the man said about her."

"Those horses were runaways, Amelia." Mother's voice was faint.

"That is not what your mother will tell us, Enid," Father said. I could tell from the tone of his voice that he wasn't as worried as Mother was.

And so we came into Riverside at a canter, not knowing what we'd find.

What we did find was Finch's wagon in the center of Riverside's biggest street, Main Street. A crowd of men were standing around it. Five men held onto the horses' reins and another man was shouting at Grandmother. Her voice rose above his. "I tell you, the horses were under perfect control all along!"

Theodora nudged me as one of the men held up his hands so Edmund could get down. Edmund had lost his hat somewhere along the road from Colton and he was pale. He saw us and began to walk over to us—not very steadily, I noticed. He sat down on the edge of a horse trough nearby as our tallyho slowed to a walk and pulled up next to the men and the Finch wagon.

Our driver called out to the man who was so angry with Grandmother. "Hey, Charlie. Keep your shirt on! Take a closer look at what the old gal's been handlin'. Look at the team Finch gave her. I think she ought to have three cheers instead of bein' chewed out. Take it up with Finch!"

The man Charlie looked at the horses. He began to laugh. "Sorry. Guess I got so mad I didn't even notice the team. Sorry, lady. Finch oughta have knowed better." He held up his arms to Grand-mother. "You're some driver, ma'am. Come on now. I'll help you down so you can go with your folks, if that's them there in the tallyho. I'll get your stuff to the Rowell, and then I'll take this here team back to Colton myself and have a little talk with Finch. I'm the sheriff."

Grandmother sat up very straight. She looked ahead as if he weren't there at all. At that moment she did look exactly like Queen Victoria. She even looked like the Queen when she moved over to the other side of the seat and got down by herself, hard as that was. I didn't know she was so spry. She came up to us and got into the tallyho without help, too. She was breathing heavily and was pale, but her voice was just the same as always when she said to Mother, "Enid, that was the sheriff! If you could have heard the things he said to me—well!"

She didn't see a man with a white mustache and a white hat pass by, but I saw him. He tipped his hat to us and looked disappointed when Grandmother didn't nod. Then he drove off down another street, but he kept looking back at us over his shoulder.

As we went the five blocks to the Rowell Grandmother kept quiet. I turned around only once and I
saw two interesting things—the sheriff driving the
black team at a safe distance behind us, and Edmund, walking, kicking at the dust of the Riverside
street. Now that it was all over I had cold chills,
even in that terrible heat. When we went inside the
lobby of the Rowell I realized that I hadn't even
taken one good look at the town that was to be our
home!

So later that hot day we left our little hotel and
walked down Main Street to the center of town.

"Oh, dear," said Mother when she looked around.

I wanted to say the same thing. Riverside wasn't
even as much of a place as Los Angeles. It had only
a couple of two-story brick buildings. One of them,
the Burt Building, had a tower and a weathervane.
It was the finest. There was another one across the
street, and I read a sign on it that said *Lyons and
Rosenthal.* I guessed that was the biggest shop.
From a sign in the window I knew that it was a
bank, too. There were a few other stores. I saw
Frankenheimer and Lightners Dry Goods. That
shop had a little card in the window that read, *But-
terick Patterns.* Grandmother, who saw it, too, told
Mother. "Look, Enid, a true sign of civilization—at
last!"

"There's another interesting sign down that way."

Mother didn't point, of course, only nodded her head. "It says *Artistic Millinery*—there in the house under those lacy-looking trees."

"Yes, and there's Fountain and Thrall Grocery," Edmund threw in. He was always hungry and had loved to go to the greengrocer's in Canada, where they sold sweets and chocolate and other good things besides vegetables. But Mother had learned swiftly that greengrocers in England and grocers in other places weren't the same, and had put an end to Edmund's spending money.

We went past A.A. Woods Hardware and J.C. Hardman City Pharmacy, but Father and Edmund stopped dead before A. Kleinschmidt's Buggy, Phaetons and Surreys, reading the sign in the window that said *Stylish Turnout*.

"We'll need a carriage, Roger," Mother told Father. Father looked pleased to have her say it before he did.

"But first of all, we *must* get out of that hotel," Grandmother exploded. She hated the hotel. Our rooms were small and hot and cost three dollars a day, a king's ransom, she told us. I knew it was expensive. Everything in Riverside seemed to be. This time I didn't want to argue with Grandmother, who still thought in shillings, half crowns, and pounds sterling while the rest of us had finally got dollars and cents straightened out in our minds in Canada.

"We'll need different clothing at once." Mother put her hand gently on Father's arm. He was wearing a gray wool suit from London and mopping at his face. So were we, in our navy-blue wool traveling costumes from Vancouver. "We're out of place here. People are staring at us."

Indeed they were. The women were dressed in white muslin, and the children we saw wore cotton. The men were wearing linen suits.

"I never dreamed the weather would be as abominable as in India," Grandmother said loudly as a man in a straw hat went by.

I looked down the next street and saw a sign on a wide, low shop that said *Riverside Ice Company*. I grabbed Edmund to show him, but he'd already seen it, and so had Theodora.

"Wish I could go in there and just sit down on a big chunk of it," he whispered.

"Me, too," Theodora agreed.

But of course we couldn't. We went on parading down Main Street, Father and Mother first, then Grandmother and Edmund, and finally Theodora and me.

"Ah, now that is what I wanted to see," I heard Father say finally. He stood in front of a shop window and I edged up, hoping they sold lemon punch there with tinkling ice in it.

But no, that wasn't what the sign said. In tall, thin black letters it said, *Algernon Somerset, Real Estate Agent.*

"This is where we shall go tomorrow morning," he told Mother and Grandmother.

And so they did. The next day, while we children watched them out of the hotel window, they set off to see Mr. Algernon Somerset. Father had read the *Riverside Daily Press* carefully that morning, so he knew something of land values. He said that he'd decided to buy an orange grove or raise grapes. The doctor in Canada wanted him to be out of doors, so he could not work in a shop or office anymore.

After they left, I read the little Riverside newspaper myself. It wasn't at all like the London newspapers. It was only a few pages long, and it had some strange things in it—for one thing, a list of all the people arriving in town each day and all of the people leaving. I couldn't imagine the London *Times* printing that or putting in a list of names of the people who had letters waiting for them at the post office.

We three didn't have to wait too long. Father, Mother, and Grandmother came back looking happy. Mother hugged the three of us.

"We've been very fortunate," Father told us. "We have a place to live and an orange grove, too. It was Mr. Somerset's own place, but he's leaving for San Francisco in just a few days. His mother, who is very old, wants him to go there to live."

"We own nine acres," Mother explained. "The place has a grove of beautiful orange trees."

"Washington navels!" Father added.

Theodora and I looked at one another. We knew what a navel was, but did people here in California talk about them straight out?

Edmund said what I was thinking. "Oranges don't have belly buttons!"

"These oranges just happen to have them," said Grandmother. "And now we shall consider the subject closed. You know how I feel about low talk, Edmund."

Mother spoke now. "Washington navels are a new sort of orange, children, the best sort to have. There's a fine house with eight rooms. It's cool and green there in the grove. We have shade trees, too, those pretty lacy pepper trees, and we have a garden and a well."

"And a canal." Grandmother looked hard at us. "The children must be told about the canal. It is not shallow. You must be very careful of it."

A canal on our own land! "Oh, we'll be careful,

Grandmother," we said all at once. But my sister's eyes were shining, and I knew that my bother was thinking of sailing boats.

"Did the house and the grove cost all of our money?" I asked Father. I wanted a carriage, too.

"No, Amelia. We have some money left in the bank in Vancouver." He smiled at me, and he didn't call me the "household worrier" this time.

"What was Mr. Somerset like? Was he English?" Edmund asked.

"He has an English name," put in Theodora.

"He was a very fine gentleman," Grandmother answered us, "even if he wasn't English. His parents came to this country from England and he'd lived in Kingston, Ontario, as a lad. Because we were English, he made your father a special and a very good price. Several men who were talking with Mr. Somerset told us we drove an excellent bargain to get such fine land for a good price during a boom period in land values. Of course," she added shrewdly, "Mr. Somerset was glad to find someone who would buy his property before he left town, so that he wouldn't have to pay another real estate agent to sell it for him."

"Of course," Father agreed.

"Tomorrow afternoon we move to our own grove," Mother told us. "Mr. Somerset is going to move

out right away. We can do our packing tomorrow morning."

Grandmother looked at the flowery wallpaper of
the Rowell and pursed her lips. "And none too soon,
Enid. As for now, we are wasting our time here in
the hotel. We must buy some light fabrics and patterns and a sewing machine today. If we don't, we'll
all melt in this dreadful climate. While you move us
into the house, I'll make new clothing for all of
us."

Mother and Grandmother left the hotel, and I
asked Father, "How do you feel?"

"A little weary, Amelia." He sat down and sighed,
but he seemed happy enough. Then he smiled at
me. "I'm not ill again, if that's what you mean, dear.
You'll like the land we bought. Don't you children
want to name it?"

Houses were often named in England, but we'd
never named our house on Nightingale Close. Father and Grandmother Thorup hadn't been able to
agree on a name for it.

Theodora surprised us all. "They don't name the
houses in Canada, so I don't suppose they name
them here. They just give them numbers. But we
can have our own secret name just the same. I know
one that even Grandmother Thorup will like."

"What's that?" Father asked.

"Well, it's a grove, isn't it? And we're still English, aren't we?" Tears came to her eyes. She wiped them away with her knuckle. "Let's call it the Queen's Own Grove."

"That's a perfectly fine name, Theodora," Father agreed. "Your grandmother will be delighted."

And so she was.

Five   The Unexpected Hesketh

THE NEXT AFTERNOON we hired a carriage and a wagon—a safer one—from Riverside's livery stable, and this time we drove south along Magnolia Avenue, a pretty street lined on both sides by pepper trees. Mother had been told it was designed to resemble the Royal Mile at Windsor.

We three liked the place we called the Queen's Own Grove at once.

The house was big, but not at all like our London house. The first story was made of adobe. That was the brown stuff we'd seen in Los Angeles, but here the adobe was painted white. Abovestairs the house was wooden. It was set back in a little forest of small, round-topped green trees. There were some oranges still on the trees in the dim grove, but it wasn't the orange season now, Father told us. He liked the grove, too. There was a bench in it, and that's where he intended to do his resting to get over his consumption.

Father told us what Mr. Somerset had explained to him and Mother about orange growing. Washington navels, the new oranges from Brazil, had first been grown in the United States in Riverside sometime in the 1870's, around ten years back. They were picked in February and March. By June all of the good oranges were gone and those that were left weren't worth eating. In Riverside there were no oranges at all in the summer, but we did have a few Valencia trees that would bear oranges in time to be shipped off at Christmas. That seemed strange to us. We always thought of summer as the time for fruit in our greengrocer's shop in England.

Grandmother, my brother, my sister, and I took a walk around our grove because Mother said we children would be underfoot in the house. First, of course, Grandmother showed us the dangerous canal. It *was* deep and the water flowed fast. Every now and then there was a place in the canal where you could pull up a block of wood, which let water run down a trench dug between the rows of trees.

"That's how we water the oranges, I guess," Edmund commented.

"That is how we *irrigate!*" Grandmother told him as she dragged us over to the well, far from the fascinating canal. Then she showed us the little garden of green vegetables and strawberry plants. I kept fanning my hand in front of my face, trying to get some cool air, until she told me to stop. I wished we could go back into the grove where it was more pleasant.

Finally Grandmother Thorup let us go in the house through the back door—"the tradesmen's entrance," Theodora whispered with a sniff. I was angry about that, too. Here we were—Bromfield-Browns—coming into our own house for the first time, and by the back door.

The house had a closed-in, screened back porch, and a big kitchen with a pump and a great black stove that looked sinister to me. The parlor was narrow and cool and dark; so was the dining room. I was surprised to see some furniture in the rooms— chairs and tables and moreen-covered sofas. We walked past Father, who was unlocking a trunk, and went abovestairs. There were five bedrooms. All of them were large and had wide windows. There was a big brass bed in one of the bedrooms, too, and a nightstand.

Grandmother explained, "Yes, we bought Mr. Somerset's furniture—what there was of it. Horrible as prices are here in this godforsaken place, we'll have to buy more today! We'll need bedsteads and mattresses and pillows." She waved her handkerchief at Edmund, who'd thrown open a window and was looking at the roof to see if he could climb out. "Come along now, children. We'll go back to town with the driver."

And so we all went back belowstairs again, where Father gave Grandmother some money and told her to buy what we needed. Then the four of us went back to the wagon.

Just as I climbed up, I saw something out of the corner of my eye. It was a round brown head popping out from behind a walnut tree not twenty feet away. Another head just like it poked out below it, and so did another—but this one had pigtails on it. Edmund saw them, too, and I nudged Theodora.

"Who is it?" she whispered to me.

"I don't know." I stared and then I said, "I don't think I want to know," as one of our watchers stuck out her tongue, another one crossed his eyes at us, and the top one put his fingers into his ears and wiggled them.

"Yah-yah!" whoever they were yelled at us, as we drove off.

Grandmother couldn't help but see them, too, after the "yah-yah." "Absolutely disgusting," she said to the driver. "Who were those perfectly revolting children?"

The driver sighed. "The Appelbooms, ma'am. They're your neighbors. I don't know the names of the Appelboom youngsters. Too danged many of 'em to keep straight, if you want the truth. Sure hope you don't have no trouble with 'em."

"Why should we have trouble?" Grandmother asked.

"Well, most folks does. The Appelbooms is a little peculiar. Wait'll you meet Pony Boy."

"Who's that?" Edmund wanted to know.

"I dunno his real name, if he's got one. That's what his maw calls him, too. He thinks he's a horse."

"Oh, dear," said Grandmother. "He sounds demented."

"What's *demented*, lady?"

"Insane, mad—crazy." Grandmother was so surprised by the question that she answered it. Usually she wouldn't answer if a question came from a member of the "lower classes," unless, of course, it came from one of our servants.

"Well, that's what folks hereabouts says about the Appelbooms." The driver didn't even know that he'd been honored by Grandmother.

"We shall have to deal with the Appelbooms, then," came from Grandmother.

The driver laughed, and got his team into a trot. I kept on thinking about our neighbors while we went down Magnolia Avenue.

Grandmother argued at the furniture shop, but finally bought enough brass bedsteads and mattresses and arranged to have them delivered out to the Somerset place at once. We had to giggle at the mistake the shopkeeper made when he gave her the receipt. "Thanks, Mrs. Stirrup, for your trade," he told her.

She stiffened as if a bee had stung her. She said, "My name is Thorup, my man—not Stirrup!"

He grinned and said, "Yes, ma'am!"

Grandmother had bought a parasol the day before when she and Mother had got patterns and cloth, and just as we left the furniture shop she opened it—right into a man's face. She was so angry at the shopkeeper that she hadn't noticed the man at all.

He noticed her, though. "Have a care of that, please, madam!" he told her in a high, clear voice. The accent was exactly like ours—English.

Grandmother lowered her parasol at once. She looked at the fair-haired man in the white linen suit who stood in front of her. He had blue eyes, a yellow mustache, and a nice smile as he took off his hat.

"Good day, Amanda," he said, to our astonishment, and then nodded to the three of us and went on his way, his hands in his pockets, whistling cheerfully.

I thought Grandmother might faint. She leaned against the front of the furniture shop while I fanned her with my handkerchief.

"Throw a glass of water on her," Edmund suggested.

"Who was it? Was that somebody we know?" Theodora was more interested in the stranger, and so was I.

"Who was it?" I asked Grandmother.

I could barely hear her reply, "That was *Hesketh!*"

And that was all she would tell us. She came to herself and sent Edmund to the livery stable to hire a carriage to take us back to our grove. How we wanted to ask questions, but we didn't dare! Who was Hesketh? Grandmother had turned green when she saw him, and she was looking more green by the mile as we headed for our new home. She looked to me as if she'd just had news of Queen Victoria's death. She didn't say a word when the driver went too fast. She didn't even have anything to say when an orange thrown by still another Appelboom, one we hadn't seen before, sailed past us as we went inside our house.

"I am definitely unwell," Grandmother Thorup told Mother, and right then and there went upstairs. She kept shaking her head and muttering to herself as she went, and I noticed how she leaned on the railings, too.

"A touch of the sun, I suppose," Father said. He and Mother were sitting down among the opened trunks having tea.

"No," my sister piped up. "It isn't the sun. It's somebody called Hesketh."

"And he called her Amanda," I added.

"She almost poked out his eye with her parasol," said Edmund.

Our mother and father acted quite strangely. Mother said, "Oh, dear—not here—not in River- side!"

Father laughed. "So Hesketh's come here, has he?"

"Who's Hesketh?" the three of us asked at once.

Mother looked helplessly at Father. Then he said, "Well, Enid, they're old enough, aren't they, to be told about the skeletons in the family closet?"

"He wasn't a skeleton. He was real as can be, and he looked like a nice man," Theodora protested.

Father laughed again. He explained to us while Mother looked down into her teacup. "That was your mother's cousin, Hesketh Thorup, I suppose. He's the only Hesketh I've ever heard of." He paused for a moment, took a sip of tea, and went on. "Hesketh Thorup is a remittance man."

"Oh," I said. I drew back. I'd heard of remittance men, of course. I knew that they were Englishmen from good families who had had to leave England.

"Did he rob the Bank of England?" my brother asked hopefully, his eyes shining. That was the first time I'd ever dreamed that Edmund knew anything about remittance men, although he wasn't really right about them.

"Oh, no," said Father. "Remittance men aren't the sort of people who must go to jail to pay for a crime."

"No, generally they are people who disgrace their families," Mother put in.

"How did Hesketh Thorup disgrace us?" I asked.

"He didn't disgrace the Bromfield-Browns, Amelia. He disgraced the Thorups. The Thorups told him to leave England. If he didn't go, they wouldn't give him any family money. If he went away, they would. So Hesketh went abroad," Father told us.

"What'd he do?" Edmund wanted to know.

"He got married," Mother said softly.

We three looked at one another. Didn't everybody get married? We'd hoped to hear something horrible!

"Why is Mr. Thorup here? Isn't it strange he's in Riverside, too?" I wondered.

"No, not so strange when you come to think about it, Amelia," Father told me. "He was told to take himself and his 'mistake' out of the British Empire entirely. By coming to the States, he wouldn't have to learn a foreign language."

"Did he come here because he had a bad chest, too? Was that his mistake?" Theodora was anxious.

"No, it wasn't Hesketh's chest that made him leave the Empire, Theodora." Father was smiling. He knew she was a "household worrier," too. "It was his head and his heart."

"His head and his heart, Father?"

"Yes, he lost them both, Theodora."

"At the same time!"

"At the same time—to an Irishwoman. She was Hesketh's mistake."

I sat down with a thump on one of our new Somerset chairs, a dusty, rickety one. I knew now why Hesketh Thorup was a remittance man. He had married "outside!"

"No, it's no great coincidence that he's here in

southern California," Father repeated slowly. "It would be a logical place for him to come, with the Empire closed to him." He touched his chin. "So Hesketh's here. That's very interesting."

"Who's the woman he married?" My brother blurted out loud the question I wanted to ask.

Mother put her finger to her lips and pointed up-stairs. "Please don't ever say her name in front of your grandmother. She was Katherine Flanagan."

"Is she here with him?" I asked.

"I imagine so, Amelia," Mother said.

Just then something thudded against the house and Mother got up and went to the door. "What was that?" she asked.

I thought I knew. I was already at the window looking out, and I saw the flick of a red skirt and a blur of bare feet going behind a little house not far away. "It was another orange being thrown at us," I told her. "It was an Appelboom."

"What's that, Amelia, a new kind of orange?"

"No, it's our new neighbors," said Edmund. "They're terrible."

"What a very odd way to act," Mother said, pour-ing more tea and offering me a biscuit.

"They're peculiar people." Edmund looked gloomy. "Grandmother says she'll deal with them."

Father nodded. "I believe she will, Edmund. But

it seems we might have Hesketh to reckon with, too."

"Oh?" I said, interested.

"Yes, Amelia, *oh* is the proper word. You see, the Thorup who told Hesketh to leave the Empire was your Grandfather Thorup." He sighed, and I thought that all at once he looked very tired and sad.

It was Theodora's turn to say "Oh." Then she added, "I hope Mr. Thorup doesn't hate us. I don't hate him, and after all, we're only half Thorup."

Now we heard the crunching of wagon wheels and Mother went cautiously to the window. "The beds and mattresses have arrived." She spoke to the three of us. "Go outside to play, children. We'll call you soon. The man with the wagon will help us assemble the beds."

We didn't dare disobey, but Edmund was looking hard at me. I knew he was thinking about the Appelbooms outside. I led the way, but stopped in the kitchen to whisper, "We'll stay close by the kitchen door."

"That's a good idea, Amelia." Theodora's eyes were round with fright.

We sat on the steps wishing that we had something to eat. The biscuits at tea hadn't filled us up much. We knew we'd have to go back to Riverside for supper, for there were no groceries in the house yet. I looked up at a little orange on a tree not far away. Nobody had bothered us; we'd sat on the porch steps for ten minutes and hadn't seen anyone. Because I was the oldest, I had to take the first chance, so I got up and walked over to the tree.

I had my hand up to the orange when all at once something hit me so hard in the side that I doubled over with pain. Another orange, a hard, dried-up brown one, lay in the dirt of our grove beside the orange I just picked.

"Limey! Limey! Dumb old Limey!" somebody yelled. Then they all came out in plain sight as I ran back to the steps, holding my side.

Edmund and Theodora had jumped to their feet. They stood up for our rights, because I couldn't talk just yet. "Who's a Limey?" Edmund demanded of the six Appelbooms.

"You are. All of you English are Limeys. You're lime-juicers—that's what my father says," yelled the tallest and oldest Appelboom, a boy. He looked about my age. He was wearing dark blue cotton trousers and a pale blue unironed shirt, and he had half a dozen hard little oranges in his hand.

So did the brown-eyed girl next to him, whose long brown hair hung in thin pigtails. Her feet were as bare as her brother's. "We whipped you Limeys way back in 1776," she hissed at us through her teeth.

"We beat you in 1812, too!" yelled another girl.

There was a boy who I guessed was just about Theodora's age. "We whipped you at the Battle of Bull Run, too!" he cried.

"Shut up, Dunstan," said the oldest boy. "That's the wrong war. They ain't Yankees, they're Limeys. The Limeys weren't in the Civil War."

The next-to-youngest Appelboom was a boy with very long brown hair. He glared at us, pawed in the dirt with both feet, and didn't say anything, but he whinnied. I guessed he was Pony Boy.

"You go home," said the last of our neighbors, a little girl with no front teeth and uncombed brown hair.

"That's the ticket, Odelie," said her oldest sister. "You tell 'em good!"

Odelie grinned and said again, "You go home!"

"Go back to England!" the biggest boy yelled at us. "Us Americans don't want you Limeys living next door to us. You Limeys are dumb and stupid!"

"That's right, Harold," said Dunstan. "They're sure stupid."

By now I'd found my tongue and I had something to tell the Appelbooms, who were six against our three. "We won't go anywhere just because ragged savages like you say so. We aren't stupid either!"

"Sure you're stupid," Harold told us. "Everybody in Riverside knows about you. Nobody else but a Limey'd be dumb enough to buy that old crook Somerset's white scale grove!"

"White scale?" I repeated.

"Yeah, that's what I said, stupid! Somerset's old grove has the worst white scale in town. He didn't even try to fight it—he just sold it to you. Your orange trees'll all be dead in three years, and then where'll you be? Old man Somerset knows all about it. That's why he's already skipped out of town. He knowed there's nothing anybody can do about white scale but find some sucker to take his grove off his hands. He sure found some Limey suckers, too."

Harold roared out laughing as we ran inside the house for safety. The hard oranges rattling behind us on the door sounded like heavy hail. I felt sick. Could what Harold Appelboom said be true?

"I think we'd better tell Father," were my only words.

Six   𝔅𝔦𝔩𝔩 𝔏𝔢𝔢

I TOLD FATHER and Mother what our American enemies, the Appelbooms, had said. Father wasn't at all happy when I'd had my say—neither was Mother. They both looked at their hands for a long time and then Father said to her, "I suppose it's too late now to do anything about it, Enid. Somerset has our money—and we have his grove."

"What *is* white scale?" Mother asked.

Father shook his head. "I have no idea, but I intend to find out." He looked at us. "Our trees still have three years of life, according to what those American children told you?"

I nodded. "Yes, Papa."

"I'll go to the bank tomorrow," he said. "They can advise me what to do, I imagine."

"Why not go see Mr. Hesketh Thorup?" I asked.

Father shook his head again. "Your mother's cousin Hesketh has no reason to like us or want to help us, Amelia. Sometimes it's better and easier to deal with strangers than with family."

"What about those men in Mr. Somerset's office?" Edmund asked, looking fierce.

Mother answered him sadly. "They were friends of Mr. Somerset's, I'm sure. They must have known why he wanted to dispose of his grove as quickly as possible."

"Crooks—more crooks!" Theodora added bitterly.

"I'd better get a book on orange growing," said Father.

I didn't say anything, although I thought we should have bought the book before we bought the grove. I wished we'd heard of white scale at least. I wanted to go out into our grove and look at the trees. Maybe I could find scales that were white. But how could I do that now? The terrible Appelbooms were out there waiting for us Bromfield-Browns!

I opened my mouth to say something about the Appelbooms, but Edmund spoke first. "They're bad people, those Appelbooms." And then he told

Mother and Father all about our new neighbors and about how cruel they were.

"Oh dear, oh dear," said Mother, "as if the heat and prices and Hesketh and something evil called white scale weren't enough, we have bad neighbors who hate us because we are English."

Then we heard a ringing voice from the stairs. There stood Grandmother Thorup, looking recovered from her meeting with Hesketh. She shouted out, "I have heard it all, Enid. We shall fight and we shall triumph! This is not the Empire, but we shall make an island to ourselves—our own England, even if it is at the end of the world. We shall win in spite of our exile!" For some reason she still had her parasol with her, and like a spear she thrust it up into the air when she'd said her last word.

"Hurrah," said Father weakly.

Mother and the rest of us said nothing. I thought that even Grandmother would have her troubles triumphing over the Appelbooms and white scale.

We three kept inside the rest of that first week in the Queen's Own Grove. It got quite tiresome. It was very hot abovestairs except at night. I thought that I could never be cool enough during the day and never warm enough at night. It was a "desert climate," Father told us. We children caught colds and wheezed and sneezed, but Father didn't. He seemed quite well and spent much of his time in the grove, sitting on his bench studying a book he'd bought in Riverside about citrus fruit crops.

The Appelbooms didn't bother him. He never even saw them, he told us, but *we* knew they were there, behind their big walnut trees, just like red Indians in the James Fenimore Cooper books we'd read in England.

It hadn't done Father much good to go to the bank in Riverside. The banker knew Mr. Algernon Somerset and his friends very well. His friends had left Riverside the day after Mr. Somerset did. Everything was perfectly legal about the sale. Father couldn't get his money back. The banker told him that every orange grove in the area had white scale, though Somerset's was the worst hit. Harold Appelboom had been right. The trees would die before long, and no one knew how to save them. The only thing that could be done was to try to keep the disease from spreading by "washing" the trees.

"With soap and water?" Theodora asked Father at supper.

"No," he told her with a laugh. "Not soap and water—kerosene." He sighed. "We must have help in the grove. I can't wash all the trees myself."

"We must have help in the house, too!" came from

Grandmother. "Enid and I have made do without servants, but we must have them soon. Working in this heat is too much, Roger!"

"Yes, I agree." Father ate another mouthful of trifle, our dull dessert that night. "I'll see to it tomorrow."

Mother, who'd been looking quite sad lately, smiled. It was true that the work of the big house was too much for her. She was getting thinner, and she said that fighting the big black stove in the hot weather took away her appetite. We always worried in our family when anyone seemed peaked. Each of us thought of one thing—consumption!

Father, Mother, and I went into Riverside the next day in our new carriage behind our dapple grays. I kept looking out the side curtains, wary of the Appelbooms, but I didn't see a single brown head that morning. Just the same I heard someone call out, "Yah-yah, Limey!" It seemed to me as if it came from the top of one of the neighbors' walnut trees. I hoped that whoever had yelled it would fall out of the tree.

We went to the only place in Riverside that hired out domestics. There were some advertisements in the newspaper, but Grandmother didn't approve of hiring from such chancy things. She wanted references.

Father, Mother, and I sat down while a woman in a blue muslin dress with deeper blue polonaise and bustle went through a stack of cards. She was American, but she was pleasant to us and didn't call us Limeys. She had listened very closely to Father when he'd told her what we needed. "Yes," she said with a smile, "what it seems you need, Mr. Brown, is a whole crew of workers—one to work in your house and several in your orange grove." She pulled out a white card and looked at it for a moment. "I believe I have the very person for you—Lee."

"Person?" exclaimed Mother. "But you just agreed we need more than one."

The woman laughed. "Lee is more than one person—a good deal more. I cannot recommend Lee too highly."

"Who is she?" asked Father.

"Lee is not a woman," she explained. "Bill Lee is his name. He is an excellent servant, and he is available only because his last master just moved to the Middle West."

"We have no need of a butler," Mother murmured to Father.

"A butler?" The woman laughed again. "Well, Bill Lee does open doors, I suppose, but he's better at cooking and housework—and he has relatives who launder and iron and work in the groves."

"Relatives?" Father asked.

"Good gracious, yes." The woman's eyes lit up. "Oh, of course, you've just come from England, haven't you? Then you aren't accustomed to the idea of Chinese help. Bill Lee is Chinese."

"Oh, dear," said Mother.

But the woman paid no attention to her. "There are many Chinese in southern California, you know. There's a Chinatown here in Riverside. The Chinese were brought into the United States some time ago to help build the railroads, and many of them stayed on in this country. They keep to themselves, but they are fine people and great workers. Bill Lee is a treasure. If you hire him, you can hire all of his relatives and friends. He will take care of the matter for you."

"What will Grandmother Thorup say?" I blurted out.

"I shudder to think," said Mother.

The woman shook her head. "You won't find English housemaids here, Mrs. Brown."

Father seemed almost pleased. "If this Bill Lee has good references, he has a position. Mrs. Thorup has lived in India. She has had Indian help."

The woman smiled a faint little smile and wrote on the card in front of her. "Ah, yes, I've heard of the *new* Mrs. Thorup in Riverside. I think she may find Chinese help something quite unusual."

As she finished writing, I caught Father's eye. He winked at me.

That afternoon Bill Lee came to us.

He drove an old dilapidated wagon up to our door and got down quickly. He was a little thin Chinese man in a dark blue jacket and trousers and a big black hat. He wore black cloth shoes, and he had a pigtail. Fascinated, we three watched him from behind our draperies as he came up to the house.

Just before he got to the door, though, an orange whizzed past him! The Appelbooms had seen him, too.

We watched Bill Lee bend over, swiftly scoop up the rolling orange, and throw it hard. Then we heard a lovely loud yell. Theodora hugged me while I jigged. "Oh, I hope he'll stay here! Why didn't we think of that—throwing things *back* at the terrible Appelbooms?"

"I don't know," I confessed. "I guess it must be because we were told never to point or to throw things."

Edmund had the same sort of answer. "We're too well-bred, that's what's wrong with us." He had his coat off again and he hadn't remembered to comb his hair that day yet, though it was almost four o'clock, time for tea. He'd kept to his room so no one had seen him. He did that a lot of the time lately.

"I'm going to cut loose pretty soon, you know." I stared at him. Where had he learned that slang? He scowled. "The trouble is that there's no Appelboom my age to fight—except girls! I've been doing some thinking. How can anybody triumph, like Grandmother says, if he can't find any enemy to fight?"

"Well, we can't fight them all at once—not when there are six of them and three of us," said my little sister, "and they only come out where we can see them when we're alone in the grove."

Then she kept quiet because Mother went past us to answer the bell and let Bill Lee in.

Father took to Bill Lee. So did we, at first mostly because he'd hit an Appelboom with the orange he had thrown. Mother said that she would take him on a "trial basis," but Grandmother said she would never take to him under any circumstances whatsoever.

Bill Lee was a good cook, even if he couldn't make a cup of tea to suit Grandmother. He made his own kind of tea, China tea, and he didn't like her orange pekoe or her Star of India tea. He didn't warm the pot properly and she kept after him until Father told her that the Chinese had been drinking tea for hundreds of years before the English had begun to drink it. After that she stayed out of the kitchen.

Our new servant could make the big kitchen stove, "the black monster," as Mother called it, behave. He could haggle in Cantonese with the Chinese vege- table men who came up Magnolia Avenue every day in their wagons. He saved us money. He knew where we could get what bargains there were in furniture and clothing in expensive southern Cali- fornia. He sometimes even sent us as far away as the town of San Bernardino. He brought his Chinese relatives and friends, five of them, to work in the groves. They washed down our trees with kerosene and water, the way Father's book said, to try to stop the white scale, but we couldn't see that it helped much.

Bill Lee didn't speak very good English. How- ever, he understood us and after a while we under- stood him. He called Theodora and me "Little Missy" and Mother "Big Missy." Grandmother was "Old Missy." She hated that. He didn't seem to have names for Father and Edmund, but he had names for all of the Appelbooms, all right. We didn't know what he called them in Cantonese, but it was enough to make Ho Lee, one of his relatives, drop a bucket on his foot out of surprise. We guessed that Bill Lee had had trouble with them before, but of course being newcomers we didn't know what, and we had been taught not to pry.

It was wonderful and at the same time sad seeing

Grandmother Thorup meet her match. All of our Irish housemaids in Chiswick had been afraid of her. They never would have dared argue with her about anything. Bill Lee never argued either. He just smiled and got his way. Grandmother wasn't accustomed to menservants where they weren't meant to be and she said this loudly and often, but Bill Lee never seemed to hear her.

Bill Lee liked us and he didn't mind if we were underfoot. He said that we were welcome in his kitchen. That was a good thing, because with the Appelbooms outside where else could we go? One day we were sitting at the kitchen table looking out the windows. Bill Lee's relatives had gone back to Chinatown and we were wishing they would come back so we could play in the grove, when Bill Lee started to talk to us about our own relatives. We were surprised. He didn't usually start the conversation.

While he rattled pots and pans he asked me, "Little Missy 'Melia, you meet Jennie and Robert yet?"

I was eating a piece of muffin and I put it down. "No. Who are they?"

"Mr. Thorup's, that's who."

"Hesketh Thorup?" Sometimes Theodora understood Bill Lee better than I did.

He beamed and nodded. "Yes, yes. That's who."

"Does he have a boy and a girl?" Edmund asked.

Again Bill Lee nodded. He pointed to Theodora and Edmund. "Same size as you."

Edmund looked thoughtful. "We've got second cousins here!"

"Wish we could get to know them," my sister put in.

I thought. "When school begins, we'll meet them. There aren't any private schools here, so no one can send us to one. We'll all go to the same school." I sighed. We *were* lonely.

"You fight with Jennie and Robert, too?" Bill Lee asked me, his eyes fixed on my face.

I thought I knew what he meant. "Not us—just Grandmother," I told him.

"I fix!" he said. "My brother work for Big Missy Hesketh Thorup. Thorups come here your house pretty soon. I fix it."

"Oh, no!" Theodora squeaked. "Grandmother will never permit it!" I knew Theodora was thinking of Katherine Flanagan Thorup—whom Riverside seemed to be calling the "old" Mrs. Thorup, though she must have been years younger than Grandmother.

Bill Lee reached for a jar of curry powder he'd ground that morning. He shook his head sadly. "Then Old Missy Thorup never be in Tennis Club!"

"What's the Tennis Club?" I'd never heard of it.

"If you no be in Tennis Club, you no be lady, you

no be gentleman—not in Riverside—you no be anybody if not in Tennis Club!"

We understood that.

"Why can't we be in the Tennis Club?" Edmund
asked. "Amelia and I can play tennis."

Bill Lee shook his head. "No! You come to Tennis
Club to drink tea, that's what you asked for—not to
play tennis—*if* you ever asked. Big Missy Hesketh
Thorup says who come to Tennis Club. Big Missy
Thorup, she Jennie and Robert's mother."

Once more we understood. "My," whispered Theodora. "Grandmother will want to be asked to the
Tennis Club."

"And she'll never be asked," I said slowly, "not
when Katherine Flanagan Thorup is the queen here
in Riverside." I felt sorry for our grandmother now.
She didn't like Riverside or its heat or anything else
about it. I knew she was homesick for England. I was
homesick, too, but I wasn't as bad off as Grandmother. Not being invited to the Tennis Club could
break her heart. It wouldn't do her much good to be
a Thorup in Riverside—not when Hesketh Thorup
and his wife had got there first.

Edmund put my next thoughts into words. "As if
white scale and the Appelbooms weren't bad
enough!"

"Are the Appelbooms in the Tennis Club?" Theodora wanted to know.

Bill Lee giggled. "No Appelbooms in Tennis Club. Tennis Club don't want Appelbooms. Appelbooms think Tennis Club full of fools. Tennis Club not American."

"What are we going to do?" I said to myself.

"I fix!" Bill Lee told us once more.

"Of course," I said, not believing him. What could Bill Lee do? It would take a miracle to clear up all of our troubles in Riverside. I wished right then and there that I were back in England, where I never would have to hear of the United States again.

"Mr. Hesketh, he come here to house," said Bill Lee. "You ask him." He pointed at me with a big spoon.

"I can't!" I was shocked.

"You write letter. He good man. He not mad at you. My brother, Sung Lee, listen him talk about you folks. He come—if you ask him."

"But what about his wife?" I asked.

Bill Lee shrugged and gestured toward the dining room door with the spoon. "Her and Old Missy just the same. Come out of same pea pod. She not come here. But Mr. Hesketh come, and Jennie and Robert come!" He smiled at me. "You like them. You write letter today. I give it to my brother."

"I'll think about it," I said. I was afraid, though.

"Mr. Hesketh big man here, Little Missy 'Melia. He help you out. He been here long time. He don't hate you. You write him, and he come with Jennie and Robert. He like come here. If you write him, I promise I do favor for you."

"What's that?" I asked curiously.

"I fix Appelbooms!"

"That's good news." Now Edmund didn't believe it either.

"When?" Theodora blurted out. She was young enough to think something could be done about our neighbors.

"Night of bad spirits, end of October—we fix Appelbooms."

"That's a long time to wait. It's only August now." Theodora was so silly I wanted to shake her.

Bill Lee seemed to be serious, though. He stirred the curry sauce. "No, not so long, Little Missy 'Dora. All Appelbooms believe in spirits. Big Missy Appelboom do what spirits tell her. She say she is 'medium.' Chinese know about spirits, too. Last night of October, Bromfield-Browns and Bill Lee fix Appelbooms. Appelbooms never bother you no more."

Now I'd almost begun to believe Bill Lee, too. "You have a plan?"

He nodded and tasted the curry sauce. "Have big bad plan for Appelbooms," he told me. His eyes grew very wide as he put down the spoon. "Curry done. Will blow off top of Old Missy's head. Hotter than India curry!"

We laughed. Perhaps, with Bill Lee's help, we *could* solve a couple of our problems.

"Tell us your plan," Edmund said.

"No. Too soon. I tell you end of October," he promised. "But now, you write letter to Mr. Hes- keth."

I was quiet for a long time.

Then my brother said, "You do it, Amelia. You write the best."

"No," I told him. "If it's going to be written at all, all of us will do it and sign it, too. Grandmother can't whip all of us."

"Not all at once, anyway," Theodora added.

"I'm not sure yet that I'm going to write it, though," I said. Then I saw Bill Lee's face. His lips were moving silently, and I could make out only one word—*Appelboom*.

That decided me!

Seven   Cousins

I DID IT. I wrote the letter that night, asking the
Thorups to Sunday tea. I knew enough to send it to
both Mr. and Mrs. Thorup, even if *she* wouldn't
come to our house. The next morning I made Edmund and Theodora sign it, too. I wasn't going to
take all the blame myself. Then in the kitchen I
secretly gave it to Bill Lee. He'd give it to his
brother, who worked for the Thorups.

"Golly," said Edmund, who kept picking up more
American expressions every time we went into Riverside to shop. "You don't need to worry about post
offices when you have Chinese servants, do you? It
seems that Bill Lee's a relative of everyone who's

Chinese in this town. Did you know a cousin of his works for the Appelbooms next door?"

I nodded, even though I hadn't known that. I was too worried about what we'd done to think about Bill Lee's relations. It wasn't at all proper for children to send grown-ups invitations to tea. I just hoped Hesketh Thorup and his children would appear at four o'clock on Sunday, and not embarrass us by writing an acceptance to Mother.

They didn't. They must have known, or perhaps Bill Lee had said something to his brother about it. Whatever the reason, we were thankful when the days passed without a word from them.

Sunday afternoon Mother and Grandmother wondered why we three were fidgeting so much, but we didn't tell them, of course. Instead, to get out of their sight we waited on the deep front porch, safely out of sight of the Appelbooms, too.

At five minutes past four the Thorups appeared, riding in a fine black carriage behind two sleek chestnut horses. We recognized Hesketh Thorup, of course, and we would have recognized Jennifer and Robert, too. They both had his blue eyes, yellow hair, and pink cheeks. They were taller and heavier than Edmund and Theodora, but about the same age, as Bill Lee had said.

Theodora ran around the house and into the kitchen before they got out of the carriage. I knew she was going to tell Bill Lee. She came flying back and whispered in my ear before the Thorups reached our porch, "He says, 'Now I fix Appel-booms!'"

We waited at our front door, hoping the Appel-booms wouldn't throw anything at the Thorups or go, "Yah-yah!" Either we were in luck or the Appel-booms were away for the afternoon, because noth-ing happened.

I spoke to Hesketh first. I wanted to call him Uncle Hesketh, but I wasn't that bold, so I said, "How do you do, sir. I'm Amelia Bromfield-Brown. This is my brother, Edmund, and my sister, Theo-dora."

He smiled and nodded. "I'm sorry, Amelia, that we weren't properly introduced the other day. These are my children, Jennifer Katherine and Robert Michael."

"Mrs. Thorup didn't come, too?" Theodora asked. She was trying to sound polite, I guessed, but she only sounded glad.

Hesketh Thorup wasn't embarrassed. "No, she's at the Tennis Club today. She sends her apologies."

Robert hid a grin behind his hand. It didn't make me exactly angry. It made me sorry for Grandmother. I hoped that we weren't going to have *that* kind of afternoon.

"*We* sent the invitation," Edmund told the Thor-ups.

Jennifer had a soft voice. "We know. We saw it."

Then there was quiet, an awkward sort of quiet, until I said, "Well, let's go inside now. We'll be hav-ing tea soon. We always have tea at four o'clock, so having someone drop in won't be too much of a surprise for Mother and Father." I hoped my hint would be taken.

"We always have tea at four, too—when we don't have it at the Tennis Club," said Jennifer.

I glanced at her sharply. No, she wasn't being nasty. I was afraid of that—afraid that her mother had turned her against us. Just because we'd never heard of Hesketh Thorup in England because he was a remittance man didn't mean that they hadn't heard bad things about us.

I took a deep breath and opened our door. "We have guests for tea," I said, too loudly. My voice made my own ears ring.

Grandmother, Father, and Mother were already drinking their tea. They all looked up and their mouths fell open as the Thorups came inside. Grandmother's cup froze halfway to her lips.

Hesketh filled in the silence with pleasant words. "Good afternoon. We were just passing by and saw your children on the porch. They asked us in to tea. Very civil of them, I must say."

I blessed him for his white lie.

Father and Mother got up. They recovered quickly from their surprise. "Please do take tea with us, Hesketh," Mother told him. She spoke then to Jennifer and Robert, asking their names, while Father and Hesketh shook hands. Grandmother put down her teacup with a bang and sat glaring at everyone.

The minute we were all seated, in came Bill Lee with more tea and a large plate of sandwiches, biscuits, and tea cakes—far more than we usually had. Mother and Father eyed the food, then they looked at Bill Lee—and finally they looked hard at us. Seated all in a row on the sofa, we did our best to look innocent.

"That is *quite* a display, Lee!" barked Grandmother. She knew that something was up, too.

"Yes, yes, Old Missy," he told her, beaming.

There was nothing she could say after that. Bill Lee had won again.

Hesketh took tea with sugar and cream. Then he began to talk to Mother and Father about orange growing. We listened while he told about his insurance company, too. He'd been in California since 1870 and had done very well. He owned two orange groves, but when Father asked him he said they both were infested with white scale, too. While Grandmother went on glaring at him, he and Father talked about what Riverside was to do about white scale, just as if she weren't there at all. I supposed that white scale, being a disease, wasn't proper tea conversation, but it was interesting, and I never had liked tea table conversation anyhow.

Mother kept looking nervously at Grandmother, and when Grandmother got up without a word and tramped upstairs, Mother sighed with relief. Then she spoke to Jennifer and Robert, who had been too busy eating to say much to us.

"How is your mother, dear?" she asked Jennifer.

"Fine." Jennifer took another tea cake, one with pink icing and white fluting along the sides.

"Now that's good to hear," said Mother. "Is she as pretty as ever? I have heard that she is very pretty, though I never met her."

"Mothers aren't pretty," said Robert. "They're just mothers."

I didn't agree with him. Our mother was wearing her myrtle-colored grosgrain silk dress today and her Thorup pearls. She was very pretty and I was proud of her.

"Who was that old lady who just left?" asked Jennifer.

I didn't even gasp. "Our grandmother," I replied.

"Oh, you know about her, Jennie," Robert said to his sister. "That's Mrs. Stirrup."

We all took in our breath at that, and the three of us looked up at the ceiling. What if Grandmother had heard!

"It's Mrs. *Thorup*," said Hesketh. I knew then that Jennifer and Robert had never been told about Grandmother and Grandfather's behavior to their father in England. They probably didn't even know that their father was a remittance man.

"Oh, is her name Thorup too? Well, anyway, she's the one old Mr. Mercer's stuck on."

"*Stuck on,* Jennifer—what does that mean?" asked Theodora. "You speak like Americans." And that was true. Our cousins were much more like Americans than like us.

"We are Americans," said Robert Thorup. "Papa's a citizen now, and we were born here in California. We aren't English like you."

"Jennifer, what does *stuck on* mean?" I repeated my sister's question.

"Call me Jennie and call my brother Bobby. The other way sounds funny. *Stuck on* means *sweet on.* You know about that, 'Melia."

Edmund blurted out, "Somebody's sweet on
Grandmother?"

"Yes, old Mr. Mercer is. He's one of our neighbors. He saw your grandmother drive that team of
runaways into Riverside. He likes women with
spunk."

"But we don't know any Mr. Mercer," Mother
told Jennie.

"He knows you. He drives by here a lot. Haven't
you ever seen him? He has a white mustache and he
wears a white hat all the time." Robert dropped a
tea cake onto his lap, got it again, and munched it
thoughtfully. "Funny that you haven't seen him.
He's always driving past your house. People at the
Tennis Club are talking about him and his driving
out of his way up Magnolia Avenue so much. They
can put two and two together when all he does is
talk about 'that dashing handsome Mrs. Stirrup.'"

Jennie added, "Mama says Mr. Mercer's a great
catch. He owns half of San Bernardino County.
Since his wife died a long time ago, half of the
ladies in Riverside who haven't already got hus-
bands have set their caps for him. It's strange you
haven't ever seen him."

Now I remembered the old man who had stared
so at Grandmother when we first came to Riverside.
But I hadn't noticed him driving past. We kept in-

side the house a lot because of our bad neighbors, and we couldn't see the road from our kitchen.

Father and Mother and Hesketh were talking family and England now, so Mother turned to me and said, "Amelia, why don't you take your guests to the grove?"

I sighed. I never had been able to get Mother to understand how truly terrible the Appelbooms were. We could play in the grove only when the Chinese workers were there, and today was Sunday.

The five of us got up and went to the kitchen. Bill Lee was busy at the stove. He only had time to smile and bow, and then back he went to his pots and pans.

The Thorups walked right through the kitchen to the back door and would have gone outside, but I stopped them just in time.

"Don't do that!" I told them. "The Appelbooms are out there!"

Robert took his hand off the doorknob fast. "Oh! I forgot where they lived, I guess."

"That's why we never saw that Mr. Mercer drive by," I explained. "We can't go out. The Appelbooms won't let us."

"They throw things at us," said Theodora.

"That's just like the Appelbooms all right, Teddie," said Jennie, giving Theodora a nickname, too.

"Dunstan Appelboom knocked out Bobby's front tooth at school a couple of years ago."

"That's when I was seven," said Robert. "It was going to come out anyway, but I didn't want it to come out that soon."

"Odelie bit me on the arm once," Jennie added.

"Well, you know the Appelbooms then. What're you going to do about them?" Robert asked us.

I didn't have anything to say to this but Edmund did. "Oh, Bill Lee says he'll fix them."

Robert and Jennie Thorup didn't laugh at all. Robert nodded his head. "Well, Ed, if Bill Lee says he'll fix 'em, he'll fix 'em. We'll help too if we can."

I felt happier than I'd felt in a long time when I saw that our second cousins had so much faith in Bill Lee. They knew him better than we did, I supposed.

"You know they have seances next door," Robert told us.

"What are they?" Edmund asked him.

"Mother says they're silly. Mrs. Appelboom calls up spirits from the spirit world."

"She does!" whispered my sister, coming closer to me.

"Well," Jennie went on, "she thinks she does. She has people who believe in things like that come from all around here to sit around a table in the dark in her parlor. Then she calls the spirits to come to her."

"Yes," Robert added, "the spirits tell all of the Appelbooms what to do."

"I wonder if the spirits told them to throw things at us," I said.

"Probably," but Robert wasn't sure about this. "Everybody knows the Appelbooms hate everyone who isn't a born American. None of the Chinese like them. They have a hard time keeping a Chinese servant, they're so mean to him. Our servant told us all about how mean they are to the servant they have now."

"The Appelbooms didn't like Mr. Somerset at all," Jennie told us.

"That's the first good thing I ever heard about our neighbors—their not liking Mr. Somerset," I said.

"They threw oranges at him, too, until he got himself a bulldog," Robert told us. "The bulldog bit Mrs. Appelboom."

"I wish we had a bulldog," said Edmund, "but Grandmother doesn't like animals."

"Maybe you could bite Mrs. Appelboom!" Jennie said seriously. "It's too bad about your grand-mother," she went on, changing the subject. "No-body in Riverside likes her, you know. Except Mr. Mercer."

"We know," I said sadly.

"She won't ever be asked to the Tennis Club for tea," Jennie whispered. "My mother says that she won't let her be asked. She won't tell me why. Do you know?"

I white-lied, "I don't know." And then I added another white lie, "Grandmother won't care, though." If anyone had told me when we were still living in England that I'd ever say those things to save Grandmother's pride, I wouldn't have believed it.

Just then Mother looked out into the kitchen and saved me from telling more lies. "Oh, children," she said to us, "you'd better come back to the parlor now. Jennifer, Robert, your father is ready to go."

We all came back into the parlor where we heard Hesketh say to Father, "Then it's settled, Roger. We'll see you the middle of September, at the next meeting of the fruit growers' association."

"Yes, Hesketh," said Father. "I'd like to keep posted on what is being done about white scale."

Hesketh looked grim for a moment. "Lord, how we wish something could be done! It looks bad, very bad, for us the way things stand now."

"Do come again, Cousin Hesketh," Mother told him.

He was silent for a moment while he touched his

mustache and looked up at the ceiling. "Well, Enid, there are things I'd like to say and things I'd like to do, but—"

"We understand completely, Hesketh." Mother was blushing a deep pink. "I'm glad you know that Roger and I had nothing to do with what happened in England."

"I know that. We can hope for a miracle, I suppose, or better, for a change of heart." He picked up his hat and went out the door.

"We'll see you at school pretty soon," Jennie told us just before the door shut.

From behind the draperies I watched the Thorups go, so I saw the orange come sailing lazily through the air and plop onto the top of the Thorup carriage. Hesketh and his children got inside and drove off in a hurry.

"The Appelbooms are home again," I said to no one in particular.

"Never you mind about the Appelbooms, Amelia!" I heard Grandmother's voice from behind me. "Kindly explain some things to me, child. You didn't seem very surprised to see those people, and that Chinaman in the kitchen certainly was prepared for guests. You didn't just 'happen' to see them passing by, did you? You didn't just 'happen' to ask them in to tea—did you, Amelia?"

I turned around. I'd been expecting this, of course. "We invited Mr. Thorup to tea—Edmund and Theodora and I. Bill Lee told us we had second cousins here, and we wanted to meet them."

"Amelia, I hold you responsible for this. You took a very great deal on yourself, didn't you?" Grandmother's eyes were blazing.

"I guess I did. I'm sorry," I said to Father and Mother—not to Grandmother. Then I faced her. "Jennie and Robert told us about your admirer, Grandmother."

If I thought this would calm her down, I was wrong. "Oh, him!" She was scornful, but not surprised. "You mean that fat old man who wears that terrible white hat? I've seen him drive by. Everywhere I go in Riverside I see him grinning like a Cheshire cat and tipping that dreadful hat to me. Who is that old fool, Amelia?"

Edmund answered her question. "His name's Mr. Mercer. He's the richest man in town, I guess." I noticed how closely Edmund watched Grandmother. "I think he's got even more money than the Thorups back in England."

"Humph," Grandmother snorted. "At least, then, he's not a fortune hunter, even if he looks and acts like one—and even if he's an American!" She folded her hands in front of her and told me, "Amelia, you led your brother and sister in this piece of tom-foolery. Don't you go inviting more Riverside people here for tea!"

Our mother amazed me now, by speaking straight out to Grandmother. "We agree with you that the children should not have invited Hesketh here without asking Roger and me first, Mother, but the fact remains that they did. Roger and I found Hesketh's visit most enjoyable and we have asked him to call again. This is Roger's house. We intend to invite the people we want to see. If you do not like the people we have here, you may go to your room. We will not force disagreeable company on you, but we will not be dictated to, either."

All Father said was, "Amen to that, Enid."

As for Grandmother, she turned on her heel and marched back abovestairs. I waited until she was gone and then I told Father and Mother all about Hesketh's wife and the Tennis Club.

Mother heard me out and then said, "Oh, dear! Oh, dear!" It seemed to me that she'd said that a lot of times since we came to Riverside to live.

Eight Princess Yellow Flower

WE DIDN'T SEE the Thorups again until school started the first week of September, but we did see more of the Appelbooms. This time we saw Mr. and. Mrs. Appelboom. It was all because of the bees. A bee-keeper came around to see us late in August to ask whether we would let him move his beehives to the Queen's Own Grove, the way Mr. Somerset used to let him. We thought this quite strange. What could a beekeeper want with us?

We listened while he explained. "It's like this, Mr. Brown. I want to take my bees where the orange flowers grow. Sure, I could put my hives out in fields that have wild buckwheat and sage and alfalfa in them, but orange blossom honey's the best. The oranges get irrigated, so my bees always get nectar from orange groves. I can't be so sure of the rest of them plants." He was a tall, thin man in a calico shirt and a wide-brimmed hat. "I'd move my hives in next February. The reason I come so early is to know how you folks take to the idea of me bringing my bees here. I'll make you a good price, folks."

Mother wasn't so sure about the idea. "What about our children?" she asked him. "Will they be stung?"

The beekeeper seemed offended. "Shucks, no, lady, I'll put my hives at the edge of the grove. Bees don't bother nobody if nobody bothers them."

"I don't see what difference it makes," Edmund growled behind me. "We can't go out in the grove anyway, because of the neighbors."

Father said he'd let the beekeeper know soon, and then he shut our front door. "Well, that is something, isn't it?" he told us. "I wonder if this is customary. I'll ask our neighbors. Mr. Somerset didn't mention anything about it."

Grandmother was still knitting woolen things, in spite of the heat. "Mr. Algernon Somerset"—she barked out the name—"did not tell us anything that was of any importance. Bees are very dangerous creatures, Roger. Do ask Mr. Appelboom. Perhaps what we need with the Appelbooms is some personal contact. They may be shy—the parents, I mean. They have never called on us. Yes, do try personal contact. I think that may be the answer."

"My fist's the answer," muttered Edmund, glowering, "if I only knew which one of 'em to hit with it."

So Father went over to the Appelbooms'.

There were some oleander bushes on the edge of our property, and we hid behind them, getting up as close as we could to the Appelboom house. Before very long we saw Father come down the steps fast, and then we saw Mr. Appelboom for the first time.

He was a short, thick-set man with brown hair and a brown beard. He came out onto his front porch shaking his fist at Father. He had a very loud voice. "You get off my property, you lime-juicer, do you hear me? Don't talk to me 'bout puttin' bees in yer grove. No bee ever stays put where he ought to be. I won't have none in my grove. Heaven help you if you put bees in yourn."

Now Mrs. Appelboom, whose red hair was falling all over her face, came out and yelled. "You git outa here, Mr. Whatever-your-fancy-name-is. We don't want no bees around stingin' our fambly."

We got up from the bushes where we'd been crouching and met Father. He looked pale, and he was wiping his face.

"Pretty awful, aren't they?" Edmund asked him.

"I never knew anyone like them before, Edmund."

I thought Father was being too generous. I looked over my shoulder. Appelbooms were boiling out of the house by now.

"Come on," I cried, "let's get inside as fast as we can." And so we did. We ran.

"What are we going to do about the bees?" I asked then.

Father laughed, a shaky laugh. "I suspect we won't have bees."

Looking sad, Theodora remarked, "The Appelbooms sure make everything bad for us, don't they?"

"Yes, Theodora, they do," Father agreed.

She burst into tears. "I want to go home! I just hate it here. I want to go back to England. I don't ever want to be an American. The only real Americans I know are the Appelbooms and they're horrible. What if all Americans are like the Appelbooms?"

"They aren't, honey," Father told her. He smiled a little. "Well, *honey* wasn't quite the right word, was it?"

Theodora went right on wailing, and ran upstairs to the sewing room where Mother was.

As for my brother and me, we marched right out to the kitchen. "Do we *have* to wait so long to fix the Appelbooms?" I asked Bill Lee.

He nodded hard. "Yes, Little Missy. When last day October come—then we fix Appelbooms good!"

We started school in the very hottest part of the year, which seemed strange to me. September in England was cool and crisp or cool and damp, but we did have new muslin and calico things Mother and Grandmother had made for us, so we were better prepared for the heat.

Our school was in two wooden buildings on Sixth Street. I was in the ninth grade, Edmund was in the sixth, and Theodora was in the fourth. I'd called my class a *form* in England, but other than that school wasn't too different in Riverside, except that we didn't wear uniforms and we had the same teacher all day long instead of several teachers. Mine was Miss Elizabeth Frear Yarborough, and she was tall and pretty enough, but she didn't permit any nonsense at all. How could she? Harold Appelboom was in the ninth grade, too.

He sat right in front of me because of the alphabet. *B* came too close to *A*. I was glad he was there, though, so I could keep an eye on him, instead of having him behind me, where he'd have put my hair in the inkwell or thrown spitballs at me. I knew Harold was the one who put the horned toad in the teacher's desk drawer. He'd put it in mine first, hoping I'd scream, but I disappointed him. I picked it up in my handkerchief and put it back in his desk at recess time. It was a good thing that Robert Thorup was our friend. He'd told us all about horned toads and desert lizards the first week of school. They were all terrible-looking, but they couldn't bite.

The Appelbooms were cruel to Jennie and Robert, too. Our family hadn't had a bit of luck. Anatola Appelboom was in Robert and Edmund's room. Pony Boy was in Theodora and Jennie's. We didn't have a minute's peace. The rest of the Appelbooms, who were scattered around throughout the school, waited for us at recess and threw sand at us until the teachers had to come out and make them stop. They stuck out their feet to trip us when we went to the blackboard. The boys hit Robert and Edmund whenever they stood in line to go back inside after recess. All of the Appelbooms chased us home. That was the worst of it—we had to go home the same way they did. We couldn't run as fast as Harold and Clotilde, the next-to-oldest, could. And it was so hot that it was hard to run. Once Harold caught me and pulled off my sash. He threw it so high into an orange tree that I couldn't get it down. One of Bill Lee's relatives fetched it for me, but by that time the sun had faded its violet to pale lavender and I couldn't wear it with my sprigged muslin anymore. I hated Harold Appelboom for that—I really hated him!

After that Father drove us to school and came to get us. He spoke to Miss Yarborough about the Appelbooms, but she said she'd done all she could with Harold. "As for the rest of them," she said right out in front of me, "I so dislike the prospect of five more Appelbooms coming up to the ninth grade that I'm seriously thinking of marrying to give up teaching."

Not even Professor Trimmer, the principal, could help. He spoke to Father, too. "I have thrashed Harold Appelboom time and again. I have visited his parents—all to no avail, sir. They are taxpayers and they do not hesitate to point out this fact to me. I bear with them, hoping that Harold will improve in high school among older lads who possibly could beat the stuffing out of him. Boys of his odd character sometimes do improve, you know."

We drove home sadly that day. Anatola and Clotilde had snatched my sister's hair ribbon at noon. Her hair was a mess. Edmund had a swelling under his left eye. Dunstan had given it to him at afternoon recess. I had a big purple bruise on my arm where Harold had pinched me while we were doing sums at the blackboard and Miss Yarborough wasn't looking.

My words just came out naturally. "I want to go home. I want to go back to England!"

Then I wished I could take my words back. They

made Father look more unhappy than I'd ever seen him. "I'm very sorry about all of this, children," he told us. "I'd like to be back on Nightingale Close, too."

"Oh, it ain't your fault, Papa." Edmund's grammar was falling apart—not from school, but from the recesses. Grandmother said he was becoming Americanized all too swiftly.

"But you feel better here, don't you, Papa?" asked Theodora.

Father nodded, but kept his eyes fixed on our team of grays. "Yes, every day I get a little better. That's what the doctor here says Riverside is doing for me." He sighed. "It looks, doesn't it, as if we're going from one bad thing to another—from the White Plague to white scale."

No one laughed at his little joke. On top of our Appelboom worries, Father had gone to the meeting of the fruit growers' association the evening before and had learned that nothing had been found so far to help get rid of white scale.

I watched a Chinese laundry boy going by with bales of laundry on each end of a long pole. I recognized him, of course. He was another one of Bill Lee's cousins.

"I wish October'd hurry up and get here," I muttered.

"Boy! So do I, 'Melia. I can hardly wait," my brother whispered fiercely.

But worst of all was the discovery I made that night, after the three of us went to bed. I never would have found out that Grandmother knew about the Tennis Club if we hadn't had ham for dinner. It was a very salty one, and I needed a glass of water, so after a short time in bed I started downstairs. I had just reached the landing when I heard Grandmother's voice.

"I gather that the Casa Blanca Tennis Club is rather important," she was saying to Mother.

"Oh, I'm not so sure of that," Mother said soothingly. "You know how such things are."

"I *used* to know, Enid." I heard Grandmother Thorup sniffing a little. "I knew it in London."

Mother said, "Now, Mother, don't take on so. No social club is *that* important."

"You know very well that it is, Enid. The Casa Blanca Tennis Club is—here in Riverside. Oh, how different things were in London!"

"Perhaps you can join, Mother. We may get to know some people who belong."

"That Flanagan woman will see to it that you and I shall never be members!" Grandmother said bitterly.

"Let's have a nice hot cup of tea. It will make you

feel better, dear." Mother was trying to comfort Grandmother, who didn't want to be comforted.

"Not even a glass of brandy would do that, Enid. Only one thing would make me feel better—leaving this terrible part of the world." More quietly she added, "But that's quite out of the question, and I know it."

"Well, I'll make us some tea just the same. Come out into the kitchen with me."

"All right, if you insist." Grandmother's words didn't have any life in them at all, but her next words certainly did. "I'd like to stone that woman Hesketh married! I'd like to stone her!"

I went back upstairs when I heard the door shut behind them. It didn't seem that I was going to have any water after all. Although Grandmother sounded like her old self when she talked about throwing rocks at the other Mrs. Thorup, she was still very unhappy.

It seemed to us that October thirty-first would never come. No matter how we coaxed Bill Lee, and we coaxed him hard whenever the Appelbooms were especially terrible to us, he'd never say one word about his plan. All he would say was that Halloween was coming!

We had to ask Jennie and Robert about Halloween. We knew it was a holiday of some kind be-cause everyone at school was so excited about it, but we had never heard of it. Our cousins told us it was an old, old holiday that had been forgotten in England. It was the night for children to have fun and to do bad things to grown-ups.

"Oh, we couldn't do anything bad—not to Father and Mother!" Theodora told Robert.

He scowled at her. "How about that mean old grandmother of yours? The one who went upstairs when we came to tea." The Thorups didn't like Grandmother, and they knew that their mother didn't like her either, but they still didn't know why. We certainly weren't going to tell them. They were our only friends at school. The other kids didn't mind our being English and they wanted to play with us, but they were too much afraid of the Ap-pelbooms to try.

"No, we're not going to do anything bad to Grandmother either," I said to Robert.

Grandmother wasn't herself anymore. She was the one who'd found Riverside on the map, and I knew that she was sorry she had, even if she didn't come right out and say it. She had less to say all the time. Sometimes she didn't even leave her room ex-cept for meals and tea. She didn't quarrel at all any-more with Bill Lee. She said that Mr. Mercer still drove past, but even that didn't make her angry. No, we mustn't play any pranks on Grandmother. Mother and Father were worried about her, too.

October thirty-first was a windy day. The norther came blowing dry and dusty out of the mountains above San Bernardino. It made our eyes water and our hair was so full of electricity it stood right up on end. Our grays hated northers. We could tell by the way they pranced and switched their tails. I hated them, too, and so did Mother because the wind blew dust inside the house. Once I barely closed the door in time on a big yellow-brown tumbleweed that came rolling and bouncing up onto our porch just as if it were alive.

When we came home from school that day, we went right to the kitchen and pestered Bill Lee about his plan. But he still wouldn't tell us a word. Finally, at dusk, he called the three of us into the kitchen.

"Spirits talk to Big Missy Appelboom tonight," he told us. "People come Appelboom house. Wing Lee, he tell me." Wing Lee was his nephew, the Appelbooms' houseboy. "You stay up late tonight!" He pointed to Edmund and me.

"What about me?" Theodora wailed.

"You wait in kitchen, Little Missy."

"That isn't fair!" she cried.

"Appelboom kitchen! You wait there!"

"Oh!" My sister smiled now. Theodora could go from sobbing to smiling faster than anyone I'd ever known. She jumped up and down. The idea of being in the Appelbooms' kitchen pleased her. "What're we going to do?" she asked Bill Lee. "Are we going to fix the Appelbooms tonight?"

"Tonight—*we fix!*" he said to us solemnly. And then he told us about his plan. It made my blood run cold, it was so dangerous, but just the same it was wonderful.

"What a way to spend our first Halloween in the United States!" my brother said admiringly. It was easier for him to talk that way—his part wasn't half as dangerous as mine. Being the oldest wasn't always such a good thing.

"Can't tell even Jennie and Robert. Can't tell anybody ever. Nephew Wing Lee lose job if you tell. He need job—even Appelboom job. You promise!"

"I promise," I said.

"So do I," Edmund told him.

"Me, too," came from Theodora.

We stayed up until ten o'clock. It was easy for me to stay awake. I was too excited to sleep. I looked out my window all the time, watching the carriages and wagons come to the Appelbooms'. I watched the lamps being blown out in all of their upstairs bedrooms. That meant that Harold and the others had gone to bed. Staying up later than they did made me feel quite superior to them.

At ten o'clock I heard Edmund going downstairs. Then I went to fetch Theodora. We crept through the dark rooms to the kitchen.

The room was lit by a single kerosene lamp. Bill Lee had one of our white sheets with him and a bag of flour. He told Edmund to hold his breath and then he powdered his face, but he didn't powder mine, or Theodora's, or his.

"What if it doesn't work?" Edmund asked him, sneezing. "What if we get caught?"

"Whipping—that be all for you. Maybe Wing Lee be fired," said Bill Lee.

"Oh." I'd expected the whipping, of course. I didn't think the Appelbooms would kill us—not in front of their guests, anyhow.

Bill Lee tried to make us feel happier about what we were about to do. "Don't you worry, Little Missy. Wing Lee help out. He want fix Appelbooms, too. You help him and Bromfield-Browns, if you do what I tell you."

And so we went out of our house, through our grove, and through the Appelboom grove. I shivered, half from fright and half from cold, though I was in my darkest and heaviest clothing.

Wing Lee was at the Appelbooms' back door. It was too late to go back now. My heart pounded and fluttered so I could scarcely breathe. Wing Lee was polite. He bowed to us and to his uncle. "Light went out in parlor little while back," he told us in a whisper. "That mean séance started. Big Missy Appelboom calling up spirits soon. It be easy for you, Little Missy Brown." He looked at me by the glow of the Appelboom stove. In that red light even kindly-looking Wing Lee seemed terrifying. My teeth were chattering and I put my hand to my mouth to keep them quiet. "I fix big table close by dining room door," he went on. "Empty place at table, Little Missy. One lady not come to séance, so I take her chair away. Empty space next to Big Missy Appelboom." He pointed. "You go in that way. Table very big. I put all extra leaves in it for séance. Easy to find empty place, I think. Big Missy Appelboom next to dining room door."

Bill Lee spoke to me next. "Remember, Little Missy, you be Princess Yellow Flower. Say you be dead Indian princess. If you caught, get out, yell! Then brother come to door in ghost clothes and yell too. Then we all run home like devil!"

I nodded, but I didn't want to go.

I crossed the Appelboom kitchen and dining room with Edmund and Wing Lee. Wing Lee put his ear to the dining room door, a sliding one like ours, and his finger to his lips. We listened, too.

I heard Mrs. Appelboom's voice now for the second time. "Touch hands, everyone."

Some girl inside the parlor giggled.

"Be quiet, Emmaline," she barked out, "while I call up the spirits."

Then Mrs. Appelboom's voice changed. It became high and thin and singsong. It frightened me more than ever. "Princess—Princess Yellow Flower. Come to me. Come to me."

Wing Lee touched my shoulder. He pulled back the sliding door without a sound. There was just room enough for me to squeeze through. I hesitated, but Edmund—who was staying behind, and could afford to be very brave—gave me a push.

My, but it was dark! It was so dark that I couldn't see at all. I stayed by the door for a minute until I thought I could see things. Even then I wasn't sure. When I heard Mrs. Appelboom talking again, I got down on my hands and knees and began to crawl toward the table.

She cried, "Come, oh come, Princess Yellow Flower. Come, dear little Princess!"

I wasn't ready yet, so I didn't tell her that the princess was on her way. Mrs. Appelboom's voice had come from my left, I thought, but I didn't know if the empty space was on her left or her right. Why hadn't Wing Lee told me that? I crept forward carefully, moving as quietly as I could over the creaky floor. I could hear people breathing and rustling. That was good—they wouldn't hear me coming. I hoped they weren't getting too tired of waiting for the princess. I put out my hand and touched the back legs of a chair, the chair to the right of Mrs. Appelboom. The empty place was on the left of her, then.

As fast as I could I crawled around her. While she called for Princess Yellow Flower again, I took a deep breath that almost made me dizzy and went under the table. It was a high table and a big one, too, but I didn't think I dared to sit down under it. I stayed on my hands and knees. I just hoped no one would touch me accidentally. The smell of naphtha moth powder and shoe blacking hit me in the face and made me feel like sneezing. I'd have to hurry.

Mrs. Appelboom was sounding impatient now. "Oh, Princess, Princess," I heard her call.

"Here I am!" I cried, trying to sound as much like Mrs. Appelboom as I could, so no one would hear my English accent.

"Who are you?" Mrs. Appelboom's voice floated above me.

"P-Princess Yellow Flower!"

"Your voice is different tonight," she sang out to me.

"I have a head cold," I sang back.

Someone else at the table laughed this time.

"Where are you? You seem very far away, Princess."

"I am very near you," I answered, then I thought for a minute that I might have said the wrong thing. Someone moved his feet under the table and a shoe brushed my right hand. I jerked it away and nearly fell on my face.

"Princess Yellow Flower, do you have a message for me?"

"Yes!"

"Tell me, little Princess."

"The spirit world is angry with you. You are bad neighbors."

"What?" Mrs. Appelboom wasn't singing sweetly now.

"You are not kind to the Bromfield-Browns." I held my breath for her reply.

"What about them?" Her tone was even sharper.

"Great harm will come to you if you harm the Bromfield-Browns," I went on caroling.

"We do not hurt those people."

"Your children hurt them every day." I wanted to add, "in every way," but I thought that would be overdoing it.

Then there was silence—a deep, black silence. I was anxious to end my part in the séance and get home, so I broke it. "Great harm will come to you if you mistreat the Bromfield-Browns. And very great harm will come to you if you mistreat Wing Lee!" My voice from under the table was such a lost wail that I was even frightening myself.

Mrs. Appelboom's voice quavered, "How shall we treat them, then?"

"With kindness—with love!" I sang out. I was tempted to add that Grandmother was a powerful witch, but I decided against it.

"Princess Yellow Flower, we shall do as you say." Mrs. Appelboom sounded more frightened than I did.

"Farewell, farewell," I told her, making my voice fade away. "Oh, farewell to you. Other spirits from the beyond will come to you now. They wait to speak with you."

"What spirits, oh Princess Yellow Flower?"

I was vague. "Other spirits—other spirits. . . . Wait here for them. Do not move."

I was tasting power, and it tasted fine. I wondered for a moment if I could do some other voices, but I didn't want to push my luck, so I edged forward to leave.

As I was creeping by Mrs. Appelboom, someone on the other side of the empty space kicked me. I guess she was just crossing her feet to be more comfortable, but she was wearing boots with very high heels and pointed toes and the toe of one boot got me in the ribs. When I started to move away, she put her foot down right on my hand. It hurt! I couldn't help it—I let out a scream. Then I tried to get up—but I hadn't cleared the table yet. The séance table went right up into the air with me, and I slid out from under it just as it came down with a crash.

Then everyone began to yell and scream and shout. I guess some of the chairs had toppled over, too. I got past Mrs. Appelboom's chair seconds before it banged into the parlor wall. As fast as I could I scuttled along with my head down hoping that falling pictures and crockery wouldn't hit me. Somehow I found the opening in the door and Edmund and Wing Lee hauled me through to the safe side.

"Shall I go in there and yell at them now?" Edmund asked.

"No, I think I've done enough," I told him as we hurried to the kitchen. Bill Lee and Theodora were waiting at the back door, and Edmund and I ran outside with them as fast as we could.

We didn't stop to draw a breath until we were in our own grove.

Then we turned and looked back. The Appelboom house was blazing with lights. We could hear
loud voices and the sounds of people running in and
out. We saw people come out of the front door at a
dead run, going for their carriages. One woman was
screaming and her husband was trying to calm her
down.

"It worked! It worked!" said Theodora.

"I didn't get to say *boo* to them at all." Edmund
was disappointed.

"I think I said all the *boo* the Appelbooms will
need." I guessed that I'd done my work well. People
were still leaving the Appelboom house as fast as
they could get away.

"Little Missy did just fine." The moon had come
out behind an overcast sky, just as if it knew that
our troubles with the Appelbooms were over, and
Bill Lee's grin in the moonlight was a wide one. "No
more trouble now that Princess Yellow Flower talk
to Big Missy Appelboom. Very successful séance.
Big Missy Appelboom be famous now."

We laughed and went home. After Edmund had
washed his face Bill Lee went back to Chinatown,
and we three went abovestairs. Edmund tugged at
my sleeve on the landing and asked, "Was it any
fun, Amelia?"

I thought for a minute. My heart was still beating

fast with the excitement. "I guess it was. But I didn't really like it very much."

"Good night, Princess Yellow Flower," he said slyly.

"Oh, dry up," I told him. "I don't want to be a red Indian princess anymore."

And off I went to bed, but I didn't get to sleep for over an hour. My blue serge dress and black stockings were in a terrible state. The Appelbooms had a green rug in their parlor and half of it had come off onto me. What if Grandmother and Mother saw that? I opened my window and let the green wool drift down off our roof. I had to smile at the sight that I saw over at our neighbors'. All of the lamps were lit now, but all of the carriages and wagons were gone—every one. I hoped this meant that the Appelbooms were talking to their "fambly" about what had happened. Or maybe people with guilty consciences slept better with all of their kerosene lamps lit?

Nine   Two Terrible Troubles

WE COULD HARDLY wait to see Harold and the others at school the next day. We certainly surprised Father by not dawdling one bit when he got out the carriage that morning.

But we were in for a disappointment. Not one of the Appelbooms came to school that day—not one. Jennie and Robert came up to us at recess. "Do you suppose the sheriff came and got the Appelboom kids because they were so bad and noisy last night?" Robert asked us.

"They didn't bother us one bit," I answered him truthfully.

"Yeah, we kept a good watch on them," Edmund told them.

Theodora covered her mouth with her hand and giggled, and I got her away before she could tell Jennie all about what we'd done. "You just go and open your mouth about last night, and think of all the trouble we'll get into. The story'll get back to the Appelbooms and they'll be meaner than ever to us. I think their spirits told them to stay home today."

She giggled again, but it was all right. I knew she wouldn't giggle anymore except with us.

That afternoon we went out into our grove, bold as brass, and after Bill Lee's relations had all gone home. No one bothered us. Nothing was thrown at us. It was wonderful.

"We sure solved one of our troubles, didn't we?" Edmund asked.

I sighed and looked at our trees. "Yes, but we've still got white scale to worry about." I inspected the tree closest to me. White scale looked like cotton wool, but I knew that it was little insects.

"And Grandmother Thorup isn't any happier," Theodora added. "She doesn't even want to go into Riverside anymore."

My brother was sitting on our father's bench. "Oh, something will turn up. I'm not going to think about it now. I'm going to make us a Guy."

Theodora clapped her hands. "That's wonderful! Guy Fawkes Day is only four days away! We'll ask

Hesketh and Jennie and Robert to come watch us burn our Guy. Americans don't know about Guy Fawkes."

"Sure," said Edmund, "it'll get us even with them for knowing all about Halloween when we didn't."

The more I thought about the idea, the better it seemed to me. "Let's ask Grandmother Thorup to help us make the Guy. It might take her mind off things."

And so we did. She wasn't too excited about it at first, but then she got an old shirt and trousers of Father's and a pillow case for a head and helped us stuff them with rags. When she painted the Guy's face to make him seem villainous like the real Guy Fawkes, she told us, "This is not such a poor make-shift Guy after all. I shall come see him burn. It will be something truly English in this godforsaken place."

"We're going to ask Mr. Thorup and Jennie and Robert," Theodora piped up.

"Well, then I won't come!" Grandmother sputtered.

"We won't have a Guy Fawkes Day without you," said Theodora. "We'll throw our Guy in the canal first."

But still Grandmother shook her head and said no.

Just the same I did send an invitation to the other

Thorups. I counted on Grandmother's weakening, and Mother talked to her for a while, too, before the night of November fifth.

When the Thorups arrived they came into the parlor and had punch and cake with us. Then all of us—Grandmother, too—went out into the grove, where one of Bill Lee's relations had built a bonfire.

Edmund had our Guy with him. He'd been playing with him ever since we came home from school. Grandmother had told him twice not to wear the Guy out.

Jennie walked to the fire with Theodora. "We're going to throw our Guy onto the fire and burn him up," my sister said. "Our Guy is very, very wicked."

"That's silly. He's just an old dummy," said Jennie.

"No, he isn't," Edmund corrected her. "He's supposed to be Guy Fawkes."

"Who's he? We never heard of him." Robert was scornful.

"He was a traitor to England," I explained, because I knew the most. "Guy Fawkes and some other men were going to blow up the king and the lords and the men in the House of Commons. Fawkes was caught just in time, just before he set fire to the gunpowder under the Houses of Parliament."

"When did that happen, Amelia?" Robert asked.

Their father answered, "Nearly three hundred years ago."

"Why, Hesketh! Why didn't you ever tell your children?" Our mother was surprised.

"They were born in the United States, Enid, and they will probably spend all of their lives here. I wanted them brought up as Americans."

Father nodded in agreement. In the light of our bonfire he looked very serious. "That's true enough, Hesketh, but it's not so easy to give up the old ways." He spoke to Jennie and Robert. "English children burn the Guy they make, so no one will forget about old Guy Fawkes. They punish him each year. Now, Edmund, throw on the Guy."

Edmund tossed the limp, long-legged Guy onto the bonfire. Sparks shot high up into the air way above the orange trees as the fire grew taller.

My brother and sister and the Thorups began to dance around the fire, and I heard Mother and Father singing, "Please to remember the fifth of November—gunpowder, treason and plot. . . ."

But I wasn't really watching them, and I wasn't listening to them, either. I wasn't even looking at Hesketh and Grandmother, who were, for a wonder, talking to each other.

I was looking behind them, at a row of dark figures of all sizes. When Edmund had thrown the

Guy on the fire, I'd heard a strange wailing sound. The Appelboom children were watching us celebrate Guy Fawkes Day. I waved to them and began to go toward them. I wasn't afraid now. Maybe they'd like to come to the bonfire, too.

But the minute they saw me coming they broke and scattered like rabbits. I heard one of the girls screaming and then I heard their back door bang shut.

I stopped at the edge of the Queen's Own Grove and laughed. Of course, the Appelbooms wouldn't know a thing about Guy Fawkes Day! We must have frightened them terribly when they saw us throw what looked like a man onto a fire and then dance around it. Perhaps they thought we were burning one of the Bromfield-Brown enemies.

We never did know what the Appelbooms thought about our November fifth, but the next day at school Clotilde and Harold came up to me at recess. I waited for them to say something, and when I was just about to walk away, Harold asked me a question. "You kids want one of our cats?"

"We got lots of 'em—kittens, I mean," Clotilde explained. "Now that Mr. Somerset's mean old bull-dog's gone, we got ourselves cats again."

"I'll ask my mother," I told them, and then I did walk off.

That night they knocked at our front door, and

there all six of them were. Anatola was carrying a kitten, a sooty, pure black kitten with golden yellow eyes.

"Here you are," she told me, shoving the kitten onto me, and then they all ran down off the porch. Pony Boy stopped at the bottom of our steps, threw back his head, and whinnied. Then he waved his hand and pranced off.

"How extremely peculiar!" said Father. "What odd children."

Grandmother had been at the door, too. "Most singular," she said.

"Not singular when there's six of 'em." Edmund wasn't good at big words.

I took the kitten to Mother, who'd already given us permission to have one. It curled up in her lap and promptly fell asleep just as if it knew it looked fine on her purple velvet skirt. "What shall we call her?" she asked.

Bill Lee came in then to tell us supper was ready. He heard Mother's question, and for a long moment he looked at the cat. "Oh, oh," he complained, "much trouble ahead in kitchen for Bill Lee. Plenty mischief there."

"That's what we'll call the cat—Mischief Bromfield-Brown," I said.

Father sighed, then he laughed. "Well, I certainly hope that black kitten isn't a bad omen for us. I'm going to a fruit growers' meeting after supper. Hesketh says a man is coming to talk to us about white scale. Let's hope he has something favorable to say."

"What does Hesketh think?" Grandmother asked him.

"Hesketh is hopeful."

Grandmother nodded and put down her crochet hook. "Trust Hesketh."

I saw Father smile at me over Grandmother's head, and I winked at him. I was a little bit hopeful, too.

The next morning when I came down early to feed Mischief, who'd slept in the kitchen, I was surprised to find Father and Mother already up. Both of them were still in their nightclothes, and they were drinking tea. Bill Lee always banked the stove fire at night and Mother had been able to get it going in the morning without any trouble. A plume of steam came from the spout of the teapot.

My teeth chattered as I took the kitten out of her warm box. We either roasted or froze in our half-adobe house.

"Come and sit down, Amelia," Father said to me.

"I'm sorry," I told both of them, "I didn't know you were up."

Father's face was flushed and his eyes bright. Now I was afraid. "Are you all right?"

"Yes, household worrier, I'm fine," he told me. "We're going to lose Hesketh for a while, though."

"Is he going away?" I wasn't happy to hear this. He was our only friend in Riverside.

"Yes," said Mother, "he's going to Australia, but Jennie and Robert and his wife will stay behind."

"He's being sent to Australia," Father explained carefully. "The fruit growers are sending him."

"But why?"

"Sit down and I'll tell you about it while your mother starts breakfast."

With Mischief purring in my arms and licking my hand with her rough little tongue I sat down across from Father.

"You know, of course, about all the ways we've tried to get rid of white scale. Kerosene and resin washes won't kill it. Steam and heat don't affect it, and if we fumigate we kill our trees. Recently we've learned that not even caustic soda will kill the eggs of the pest, although it will kill the bark and burn the leaves of the trees."

I nodded. We hadn't tried that, but other growers had. "I know, Papa," I said. "I know we only have three years to get rid of it—or else."

"That's right." Father was really excited. "The

man from Washington, D.C., told us last night that the home of white scale is Australia."

"Then why send Uncle Hesketh there?" I couldn't help but say. "Isn't there enough white scale in his own grove?"

Both Father and Mother laughed at me, and then Father went on between sips of tea, "White scale exists in Australia, Amelia, but it is controlled there. Hesketh is going to an international exposition in Melbourne to learn *what* controls it. Once we know that, we can fight it ourselves and save our groves!"

Now I was excited, too, at this wonderful news. "When will he be back?"

"He'll be gone at least three months. Australia is a long way from Riverside."

I knew that. "Maybe when Uncle Hesketh comes home and all of the groves in Riverside are saved, his wife will forgive Grandmother and let her into the Tennis Club," I said happily.

A shadow went over Mother's face. "Don't hope for too much, Amelia. We don't know whether Hesketh will learn anything in Melbourne that can help us. As for the business between Amanda Thorup and Katherine Flanagan Thorup, I still think it would be wisest to hope for a miracle."

"Yes, oranges may grow on trees, Amelia, but miracles don't," Father warned me.

I looked down at our new kitten and thought

about the Appelbooms. We'd already had one mira-
cle since we'd come to Riverside, but I didn't think
Princess Yellow Flower could help the two Mrs.
Thorups.

"I'll watch for a miracle and I'll help one out if I
see it coming," I whispered into Mischief's tiny pink-
lined ear, and the kitten flicked her ear and put out
a soft paw to touch my nose.

November, December, and January passed with
Hesketh gone to Australia. Finally February came
and we learned about who Abraham Lincoln was
and George Washington, too. I admired George
Washington even though he had fought the British
a long time ago. I didn't mention him to Grandmother, however, who still moped and was very
quiet. She certainly wasn't herself at all.

Everything was quiet in our house—too quiet for
the three of us. We only saw Jennie and Robert at
school. They said they wanted to invite us to their
house to tea, but their mother was "too busy." We
understood, but our Christmas had been lonely, almost as lonely as our Christmas in Canada had
been. That time of year was when we missed our
Bromfield-Brown relations in England most of all. It
certainly hadn't been an English Christmas, not
with the sun shining and Father out in the grove in
his shirt sleeves in the afternoon. No one came

caroling, and we didn't have roast piglet. We had a goose. Bill Lee and his relations came in and we gave presents to all of them, but somehow it wasn't the same. For one thing, they gave us fireworks in return, which seemed peculiar to us.

We. didn't see much of the Appelbooms. They were very nice to us at school, but they kept their distance at home. When we went out into our grove, they left theirs at once. So we stayed inside, looking at stereopticon slides of Queen Victoria's palaces and cutting out silhouettes. It was getting a little too chilly to go out into the grove after school anyway.

If there was one thing you could say about southern California in the winter, it was that you could never count on the weather. The Saturday after New Year's Theodora sunburned her nose. The next day she nearly got pneumonia from sitting on our wet bench.

One afternoon late in February we came home shivering. All day long a norther, a cold, dry one this time, had blown down on Riverside from the Mojave Desert. At sunset the wind died down. The sky was a clear, pale blue—so blue it was milky-looking.

Father looked at it and shook his head. "I don't like that sky, Amelia. Ask Bill Lee to come here, please."

I hurried to the kitchen, but I couldn't find Bill Lee at first. Then I heard him muttering to himself and found him standing on the back steps with a frying pan in his hand. He was gazing up at the sky, too, as if he'd never seen it before.

"Bad sky, Little Missy 'Melia."

"That's what Father just said. What does it mean?"

"Might freeze oranges on tree. Bad thing!"

Now I understood, and I was frightened. "What can we do?"

"I talk to Mr. Brown. Then I go to Chinatown and get family here. Will hurry."

Bill Lee and I went to find Father, who was still out on the front porch looking up at the sky. It was fading away to purple black night and stars were already winking down at us.

A kerosene lantern came swinging toward us from the direction of the Appelbooms, but I wasn't afraid, not now.

Mr. Appelboom came to the bottom of our steps. He set his lantern down. "Thought I'd come warn you, seein' as you're new to these parts. Would be the neighborly thing to do," he told Father. "We're due for a killer frost, less'n I miss my guess."

"That's what I thought, too," Father said. "This is the sort of weather my books on orange raising said presaged cold weather and heavy frosts."

"Don't know what *presaged* means and I don't care," came from Mr. Appelboom, "but there's nothin' worse'n a bad frost, less'n it's white scale. You know what we do about killer frosts here?"

"No. I was just about to ask you."

"Well, some of us growers flood our groves from the canal. The water'll keep the cold off—sometimes. You only got to keep your place a degree above freezin', you know. But I ain't gonna flood my place this year. No, I'm puttin' fires in my grove. I'll light 'em tonight. Why don't you give that a try, too, Mr. Brown? You folks seem to know how to build a pretty good bonfire." I knew he was talking about our Guy Fawkes fire. "Are you going to have enough help?" he asked.

"Will we, Lee?" Father turned anxiously to Bill.

Bill Lee nodded. "Yes, yes. I go get help now—get big load of wood, too."

"I laid my fires this mornin', neighbor," Mr. Appelboom went on as Bill Lee hurried around to our stable to get his horse and wagon. "My boys and I could help you out with yours if you'd like."

"That would be very kind of you, Mr. Appelboom."

I was pleased that Father had accepted the Appelbooms' offer. Now Mr. Appelboom nodded. He was pleased, too, at having done us a favor. "Guess you'd better tell your women folks that nobody's goin' to do much sleepin' tonight, Mr. Brown. You'll be needin' every hand you got to tend your fires, and somebody'll have to lug coffee around. Coldest time of all's gonna come between midnight and daylight." He looked at me. I had never noticed it before, but he had nice warm brown eyes. "Think you can stay up and help out, too, little lady?"

"I can," I promised. "So can Edmund, maybe, but I don't know if Theodora can. She's only ten."

The Appelboom boys and their father helped Bill Lee and his relatives set our fires, and then a couple of hours after supper we went out into our grove with a thermometer. We all gathered around and looked at it by the light of a lantern. It showed thirty-eight degrees at first. An hour later it showed thirty-six.

"It's falling fast," said Father. "Let's get those fires lit. Amelia, you start making hot tea."

We put in a wild, hard night. I think I carried out gallons of hot tea, going from fire to fire among the trees. My brother sat on the ground next to his fire. Like all of the other fires, it was only a red glow. I could barely find him for the smoke, but I didn't mind it—not even when it got to my eyes and stung. I knew that Mr. Appelboom and Father wanted a lot of low-hanging smoke to drift among the orange trees to keep the temperature up.

Edmund was shivering when I poured out his tea

for him. "Father was just here," he told me. "The temperature's thirty-four now, and he's afraid that the wind might come up before dawn."

I knew what he meant. "That would drive the smoke away."

"Yes," he said. "It's two hours until daylight."

I bent over and threw more wood onto my brother's fire. "Whatever you do, *don't* go to sleep," I said, and then I went on to Ho Lee's fire with my heavy bucket of tea. Bill Lee's relations could drink even more tea and hotter tea than an Englishman.

Just before dawn Father took his thermometer outside our grove and found that the temperature had gone below freezing, down to thirty degrees. We only hoped that our fires had been able to keep the temperature in the Queen's Own Grove up to thirty-three.

When the sun came up we all were still on the job, and what sights we were! Our eyes were red and our faces were black from the smoke. We were so tired when it was finally warm enough to let our fires die out that we could hardly walk back to the house.

Mr. Appelboom, looking as weary and smoke-grimed as the rest of us, came around to our back door just as Father and I were going in. "How'd ye make out, neighbor?" he asked Father.

"All right, I guess—at least I hope it's all right."
Father was almost too exhausted to speak.

"Do you know how to tell when an orange is
frozen?" Mr. Appelboom asked him.

Father shook his head.

"Well, after we wash ourselves up and put away
some breakfast, I'll come over and show ye."

Then in we went and sat, worn out, in the kitchen
while Grandmother, working together with Bill Lee
now, cooked ham and eggs and muffins for everyone. I was too tired then to think how strange this
was. Grandmother hadn't said one complaining
word all night long. She had tended her fires in the
grove as everyone else had. It was a silent breakfast,
eaten off soot-speckled plates, but no one said anything about it. Everything in the house was black-
ened with a layer of smoke. There'd be lots of
housework ahead, but right now nobody cared to
think about it.

Theodora came down, yawning and stretching.
She'd only been able to stay awake until eleven, but
she'd done her best.

After breakfast we went back into the grove
where our fires were smoldering out. I guessed all of
the other fires in Riverside were going out, too. A
big cloud of deep, gray, woolly-looking smoke hung
over the town in every direction I could see.

Mr. Appelboom came toward us. He had a large knife in his hand. How that would have frightened us a couple of months back, but we only looked at it curiously now.

Father had been examining our oranges. They looked fine to me—round and orange, just about ready for picking. "They're all right, Mr. Appelboom," said Father.

Our neighbor shook his head. "Nope, Mr. Brown, you can't tell a blessed thing by just lookin' at 'em. You know what freezin' does to an orange? It busts the orange pulp. All the juice dries up, that's what happens. Here. If your grove's as bad off as mine is, it won't be hard showin' you what a frozen orange's like."

He pulled an orange off the tree over my head, put it on our bench, and sawed it in half. "Looka that, Mr. Brown! It's froze, all right."

The orange looked strange inside. It had a pale, dead-looking color.

"Oh, dear," I said.

"Raisin' oranges is a funny business. Wish I never did get myself into it, but my old lady didn't take kindly to Missouri winters and pestered me to come out here where livin' was easier. I ain't found it no easier, what with white scale and killer frosts. It's a mean tricky business." He reached up and took another orange from the same tree. "This one could be all right."

And so it was! It looked just the way an orange is supposed to look inside—bright, golden, and dripping with juice.

"But they came off the same tree! How are we going to know which oranges are frozen and which aren't?" Father asked him.

"That's just the trouble we got, neighbor. You can't never tell. One'll freeze on a tree and the one next to it on the same branch won't. We have to pack 'em and ship 'em out, good ones and bad ones together."

"That's terrible," I said. I didn't think that was fair to whoever bought the oranges.

"You're right, little lady, it's a bad thing, but we got to do it. We sure don't want to, though. And when there are too many bad oranges in a shipment, we get complainin' from the customers. Can't say I blame 'em neither. A bad freeze and a lot of bad oranges goin' to market gives Riverside a bad name, let me tell you!"

"But there must be *some* way to tell," I heard my sister wail.

"You folks think of a way, little girl, and Riverside'll never forget you!"

Ten   The Great Discovery

WE CERTAINLY DIDN'T know what to do after Mr. Appelboom showed us how impossible it was to tell a frozen orange from a good one. The only way we could be sure was to cut every orange in the Queen's Own Grove in two, and, as Grandmother pointed out, sounding like her old self again, "That is hardly a profitable thing for us to do."

Father was upset, of course. It was hard for him and for the rest of us to believe that the growers took such a terrible chance when they sent their oranges to market. He went to a fruit growers' meeting right after the night of the killer frost and asked about it, but no one could tell him much more than Mr. Appelboom had.

Old Mr. Mercer was at that meeting, too. According to Father he came up afterwards and told Father that sometimes after a freeze we'd find dark spots on the orange tree. That could let us know that some oranges on the tree had probably frozen. It seemed that Father had had quite a conversation with Mr. Mercer. He'd liked him, and that pleased me. Riverside was a lonely place for us Bromfield-Browns. We all missed Uncle Hesketh.

"I nearly asked Mr. Mercer to Sunday tea," Father told me as we walked around our grove, "but I decided that it wouldn't be too wise."

I understood. "I know. She might go upstairs again, the way she did when Uncle Hesketh and Jennie and Robert came to tea the first time. Did he ask about her?"

"Indeed he did! He wanted me to go to the St. George Hotel to have a glass of brandy with him, but I didn't go."

"Why not, Papa?" I wished he had gone. Mr. Mercer interested me.

"Because I thought all he'd do was talk about 'the dashing Mrs. Stirrup.'"

"Hasn't he got her name right yet?"

Father shook his head. "No, Amelia. I have the feeling that once Mr. Mercer gets an idea into his head, it hasn't much chance of getting out."

"Well, Grandmother certainly isn't that way anymore. She's changed a lot. She's nice to all of us now."

"Yes, she does seem to be mellowing," Father agreed—rather sadly, I thought.

Then I had an idea. "Does Mr. Mercer belong to the Tennis Club?"

"I didn't ask him that, Amelia. We only talked about oranges and Amanda."

"You find out next time you see him," I told Father.

"Oh, Amelia." Father began to laugh. "You know better than that. He'd think I was hinting for him to ask us to come drink tea at the Tennis Club. I don't care about the Tennis Club. Neither does your mother."

"It's not you or Mother I have in mind," I said very seriously. I'd been doing a lot of thinking. Mother and Father and I were changing, and so were Edmund and Theodora. I suspected we were becoming Americanized. But Grandmother wasn't. She was old, and old people don't take on new ways easily. "It's Grandmother I'm thinking of. She needs some friends her own age. She hasn't got anyone but us. She said we'd triumph, and perhaps the rest of us will, but she won't—not at all."

"Well, Amelia, I'll try to find out about Mr. Mercer and the Tennis Club," Father promised me solemnly, "but I have no idea how I am to go about it."

The oranges were to be picked, packed in boxes, and taken to the railroad station, where they would be shipped off to San Francisco and the East, by the end of the third week in March.

A few days before we were to have our fruit picked, Father and I went into Riverside. We went to the public library just as we always did, but this time Father came home with the strangest books he'd ever taken out—a book about physics and one about chemistry.

"Whatever in the world do you plan to do with these, Roger?" Mother asked him that night.

"I intend to read them," he told her, "until I find out what I want to know."

"What is that?" asked Grandmother.

"How to separate the sheep from the goats!" he answered her with a grim look.

Edmund and Theodora laughed at his words, but I didn't. Neither did Mother nor Grandmother. Whatever reason Father had for borrowing such odd books must be a good one, and when he spoke about sheep and goats he was not joking with us.

For the next three nights he had his head in one or another of the books, but on the morning of the fourth day, a Saturday, he called to Edmund and Theodora and me to come out into our grove with him. And a few minutes later along came one of Bill

Lee's relatives carrying a big copper washtub. Two other carried buckets, which they filled from the canal and dumped into the tub.

Then Father gave each one of us a good-sized basket. "Edmund, you take an orange from every fifth tree on the east side of the grove. Theodora, you do the same thing on the west side. Amelia and I will take the north and south sides."

I counted my trees off carefully, asking myself what Father had in mind while I took one ripe orange from each fifth tree. I was getting excited—more excited all the time. Something was up!

Father was back at the tub of water before I was and Bill Lee was with him, his kitchen cleaver in his hand.

"Empty your basket into the water, Amelia," ordered Father.

I did what he asked me to do, putting my oranges in beside his. Some of his were floating. Others had sunk to the bottom. While I watched, full of curiosity, most of my oranges went to the bottom of the tub.

"See what I mean, Lee?" Father asked him.

Bill Lee was excited, too—even more excited than he'd been the night of the Appelboom séance. "It look mighty fine, Mr. Brown. If it work, you be great man!"

Now my brother and sister came up, too, and emptied their baskets into the tub.

Father and Bill Lee put a small plank over one end of the tub. Then both of them went down on their knees in the dirt of the grove. I heard Father take a deep breath. "Oh, let me be right!" he said, and it sounded like a prayer. Then he rolled up his sleeve and reached down into the tub and took out an orange. Up it came, gleaming golden and dripping wet. Father gave it to Bill Lee, who put it on the plank and with one whack of his cleaver split in two.

"Perfect—a fine orange," said Father. He reached down again and brought out two more oranges from the bottom.

Whack, whack, went the cleaver again. Both oranges were good ones.

"Try others," said Bill Lee.

Father's expression was somber when he gave Bill one of the floating oranges.

The cleaver went through this one, too, but this time the orange was dry and pulpy inside. It was one that had frozen.

"Ah!" breathed Bill Lee.

Now Father smiled—but only a little. He didn't take any more floating oranges. He took oranges only from the bottom of the tub. And each orange from the bottom turned out to be a perfectly good one.

"All right, Lee. This will be the proof of the pudding," he said. He gave Bill Lee two of the floating fruit.

Whack, whack, went the cleaver once more. Both oranges were bad ones—frozen oranges. One after another Father gave the floating yellow balls to Bill Lee, who cut them open. Every one was bad! So that was it! That was why Father had taken out those strange science books. He had learned that good oranges were heavier than bad ones.

Father got up slowly and rolled down his sleeve. He was really smiling now. "Well, I guess that proves it, doesn't it?"

Bill Lee bowed, with his cleaver still in his hand. "You great man in Riverside, Mr. Brown!"

"Thank you, Lee," Father said calmly.

As for Edmund and me, we went wild with joy. We jumped up and down and yelled like red Indians. After a while we had to stop and explain to Theodora what all the celebration was about. And afterwards I thought that my brother and I certainly hadn't behaved like proper Englishmen when we whooped in the Queen's Own Grove.

We went the same day to the Appelbooms', and while everyone crowded around Mrs. Appelboom's washtub, Father and Bill Lee showed them how to tell the "sheep" oranges from the "goat" oranges be-fore they were packed and shipped off.

"You're sure a good neighbor, Mr. Brown," said Mr. Appelboom admiringly. "You did this town a lot of good just now."

"I hope so," said Father.

"Now all you got to do is show ever'body else."

"That will be a big job, and there isn't much time before we send the fruit to market," said Father. "We could call a meeting of the fruit growers' asso-ciation, I suppose."

"Me and Harold'll help out, whatever you folks decide to do," our neighbor offered.

I thought fast. Here was our chance to meet people—lots of people. I put in, "You can split up the town and go from grove to grove, and show people how to tell good oranges from frozen ones." Then I shut up, partly because I didn't have the right to talk out of turn like that, but mostly be-cause Mrs. Appelboom was there. She might have recognized the voice of Princess Yellow Flower. I couldn't have that happen.

"A good idea, little girl," Mr. Appelboom agreed. "We'll get on it right away. Some folks are already shippin' fruit out."

A couple of times after school that week Edmund and I got to go with Father in our carriage as he went from grove to grove in the west part of River-side. I really liked it, and was glad we did that instead of calling a meeting of the fruit growers' association. We met people that way, and some of them fed us milk and cookies while Father showed off what people called "the Brown experiment." Privately Edmund and I called it "the great Bromfield-Brown discovery." We thought Father's name ought to go down in Riverside history.

We went to two interesting places on our travels. One of them was Mr. Mercer's grove. Father went to the St. George Hotel first to pick Mr. Mercer up. Edmund and I listened to them talk as they sat in the front of our carriage.

"Nice family you got, Mr. Brown," he heard Mr. Mercer say.

"Thank you, Mr. Mercer," said Father.

"Yep, sure do wish I had me a family, too. I built the biggest house in town. You'll see it in my grove today. It's stood empty for a long time. I didn't want to live in it alone after Minnie died, so I moved to a hotel. Minnie and me, we never had kids. Wish we had though—sure wish we had."

"That's too bad," Father told him. "Sometimes, though, a family can be a rather difficult thing, you know." I guessed what he meant. Edmund had been thrashed a few days back for playing too near the canal. Father was getting much stronger, Edmund said.

"Do tell," came from Mr. Mercer. "Does Mrs. Stir-rup have much of a family back in England?"

"Only some sisters—maiden ladies, all of them. Her family wasn't much for marrying. Amanda is the only one who did marry."

I wanted to poke Father. That made Grandmoth-er's family sound peculiar, and I didn't want Mr. Mercer to think that, but I didn't have to worry.

"Mm-m, Amanda!" he breathed. He made the name sound romantic. "I hear Hesketh Thorup's a relative of hers."

"Only of her husband's. Her husband's been dead for many years, Mr. Mercer."

"Hm-m." Mr. Mercer's white mustache was so wide I could see it from behind. One side of it twitched in the breeze. "So she's not got much of anybody, either."

Edmund opened his mouth. I just knew he was going to say, "She's got *us!*" but I didn't want him to say that, so I nudged him and whispered. "You let me talk to him about Grandmother."

"We'll tell Grandmother that you asked about her," I told Mr. Mercer as sweetly as I could.

Mr. Mercer was pleased. He turned around and looked at me and then tipped his hat once more. I liked that. I was wearing my green velvet bonnet with the little white ostrich plumes, and my green cloak and opossum muff, and I felt very grown-up in them, even though my skirts weren't down yet or my hair up. But I did have puff bangs, thanks to my Christmas curling iron. "Well, thank you, little lady," he told me. "Give my warmest regards to your grandmother."

"Oh, I will," I promised. Then I asked, "Do you play tennis, Mr. Mercer? Grandmother just loves it."

"Never did play the game. There's only one game I do like, little girl."

"What's that, sir?"

"Poker. I do like a good game of poker."

"What's poker?" Edmund asked him.

Mr. Mercer guffawed. "You're too young to know, sonny, but someday I'll show you how to play."

"All right, thank you," came sourly from Edmund, who was always miffed at being too young for something.

Then we got to Mr. Mercer's grove and Father demonstrated his discovery. Mr. Mercer said, "By golly!" a lot and after it was all over, he pumped Father's hand up and down.

Then he asked me if I would like to see his house. I hadn't been able to take my eyes off it, and I was dying to see the inside. It was white and it was huge. It reminded me of a cake—the biggest cake in the world. It had pillars and cupolas and balconies and deep porches and bay windows and more elegant things than any house I'd seen anywhere in Riverside.

Inside, it was wonderful. The furniture was covered with dust sheets, but he showed me the red velvet sofas and the piano and everything I wanted to see. While we walked through the house and I peeked into every room—and there seemed to be several dozen of them—Mr. Mercer kept right on talking. He told me that he had the biggest orange grove in San Bernardino County, four alfalfa ranches, two raisin grape ranches, a general store in Colton, a horse farm, and a dairy farm. I think he was just about to tell me how much money he had in the bank when Father called from outside that it was time for us to go home. I hadn't been able to find out about the Tennis Club at all, and I went home a little miffed that night, too.

Hesketh's grove came next. We went there the next afternoon. Their house was a lot like ours, but it was painted yellow. Jennie and Robert came out to meet us and so did their mother. She was a tall, black-haired lady in a beautiful blue afternoon gown with cream-colored Chantilly lace, and porcelain buttons with white roses painted on them. Her eyes were the same blue as her gown. Katherine

Flanagan was beautiful. We all gaped at her—even Father. I could see why Hesketh had lost his head and his heart to someone that pretty.

"Do come in," she said to us all. So before Father showed her the new method of orange choosing we children had pound cake and orange punch, and she had a glass of sherry with Father. Her voice was soft and lilting, and I would have liked to sit and listen to her.

"Yes, I do so miss Hesketh," she told Father. "He should be home very soon now."

"Have you heard from him, Mrs. Thorup?"

"No, Mr. Bromfield-Brown. Hesketh is not a good correspondent—as a matter of fact, he is not a correspondent at all." She sighed.

"Has he written to anyone to say if he's learned anything about white scale?" Father asked.

"Not that I know of."

"Oh, Papa will stop that old white scale when he gets home," Robert boasted.

Here was my chance. "Yes, that's what Grandmother always says. She says, 'Trust Hesketh Thorup.'"

Father gave me a hard look while Mrs. Thorup murmured, "How nice," and sipped her sherry. Somehow I didn't like her words. The way she said it, it sounded like "Too late!" or "Who cares?"

Then we went out into the grove with Mrs.

Thorup's Chinese foreman. We could have stayed behind and played with Jennie and Robert, but Edmund and I didn't want to—not in Mrs. Thorup's house. At school the next day it would all be different, but school was neutral ground. Jennie and Robert weren't like their mother.

My brother and I talked together when we went back to our carriage. Father had gone up ahead so he couldn't hear us. "I don't think Grandmother's ever going to get into the Tennis Club," I said, feeling gloomy and put upon.

Edmund kicked at a tumbleweed and sent it scudding off across the road. "It doesn't look as if she will, 'Melia."

"Well, we've had a couple of miracles already since we've been here. I guess we ought to give up hoping for more."

"Maybe so. I guess you're right. That Mrs. Thorup's going to be a tough nut to crack."

"If you think of some way to crack her, let me know, Edmund." Two heads were better than one—even if one of them was Edmund's.

"Why don't we ask Bill Lee, 'Melia?"

I shook my head. "It's pretty private business, Edmund. I don't think we ought to."

"He's a good fixer."

I thought hard about that as we went back home in silence.

Eleven   The Last Link

JUST AS SOON as I could see him alone I went to the kitchen to talk to Bill Lee. I suppose I shouldn't have told him everything, but I did. After the Halloween séance he was more to us than just a servant and cook. He was a fellow schemer.

Bill Lee shook his head when I told him about Mrs. Hesketh Thorup and Grandmother. He nodded and shook his head a lot of the time when he didn't talk. I knew by now what these nods and shakings meant. It wasn't easy for him to speak English. He'd told us that he was born in Canton, in China, and he'd learned English when he came to the United States. So I guessed that made it even harder for him to understand us Bromfield-Browns. Even though we had been away from England going on two years now, we still didn't really speak like Americans.

"Do you know what I mean?" I asked him when I'd finished.

"I know, Little Missy," he told me. "I ask Sung Lee, little brother, what he think about it. He keep mouth shut. He keep ears open. He hear things in Mr. Hesketh's house."

I hadn't really planned to have Sung Lee in on it, too, but I guessed it couldn't be helped. I'd caught a glimpse of Sung Lee in the Thorup house. He looked a lot like Bill Lee. I only hoped he was as wise.

A week went by and then Bill Lee crooked his finger at me one day when I was going out to the grove. "I talk to Sung Lee. We play dominoes last night," he told me.

"What did he have to say?" I could hardly wait to know.

"Sung Lee hear Big Missy Thorup talk one time to Mr. Hesketh. She say Bromfield-Brown family have bad manners."

"We do *not!*" I was really angry now. "What does she mean?"

"Not know, Little Missy, what she means." Bill

Lee looked puzzled, too. "That be all Sung Lee hear. Big Missy Thorup say she not come to your house when you have bad manners. All right if Mr. Hesketh come if he want to—but not Big Missy!"

"Well, I never!" I exploded.

Bill Lee giggled. "You just like Old Missy when you get mad," he said to me.

Being told I was like Grandmother didn't make me any happier. I went upstairs two steps at a time. I was so angry I could have chewed on nails, iron ones. My brother and sister and grandmother were in the grove, but if I went out there I'd be sure to say something about "Big Missy" Hesketh Thorup, and it wouldn't do to talk to Grandmother about her, no indeed! Father and Mother had taken the carriage and gone into Riverside, so I had the whole top floor of the house to myself.

For a while it was quiet except for our old hall clock, which reminded me of England and our house on Nightingale Close every time it struck the hour.

But then I heard a yell from the grove. I went to my window and looked out. All I could see were the green tops of our orange trees and a few oranges the pickers had left when our fruit went to market.

I went back to my fractions homework calmly. The yell had been an Appelboom yell. I knew them all by now. It had sounded like Anatola, she was the shrillest screecher, but it could have been Theodora, too, much as I didn't like to admit it. Grandmother permitted us to yell outside now, even when she was there reading, something she did a lot of the time.

The next yell, though, made me get up and charge downstairs and out of the house as fast as I could. I'd heard Edmund bellow, and that could mean a fight. If it was a fight I was going to be there.

It wasn't a fight at all. It was something else— something Father later called "an historic moment" in our lives in Riverside. The first thing I saw was the Appelbooms—all of them—dashing toward us through their grove along the banks of the canal. All of them, that is, except one—Pony Boy.

"What's wrong? What's wrong?" I called out to them.

"Pony Boy! Pony Boy's gone and fell in the canal!" Harold answered me.

"He's comin' right along," Clotilde said breathlessly. The hem of her skirt was all wet and so were the ends of her braids.

"Real fast," added Anatola.

"I saw him. I just saw him!" Theodora jumped up and down.

"Well, somebody do something!" came from my brother, who ran to the brink of the canal and looked up the wide deep water trough to the Appelboom property. I hurried over to where he was, and saw what he saw—Pony Boy being swept along toward us by the water. He kept rising and sinking as he came. He couldn't get out. The sides of the canal sloped too much and the current was swift.

"Golly, he sure is movin'." Anatola sounded almost admiring of her brother's speed. "We can't reach him sticking out our hands. Not even Harold can get him!"

"Somebody do something!" I screamed. "He's going to drown!" I was terrified. There was a bend in our canal about a hundred feet farther along where the water ran even swifter.

"If he gets that far," Clotilde said, pointing, "he'll be a goner for sure."

Then we all heard Grandmother's voice. "Stand aside, children. All of you!" There was no arguing with that tone. We stood aside. She looked at Pony Boy, who was sinking again. "I shall do something!"

She went to her knees with her parasol held ready in one hand, and as Pony Boy came abreast of us on the current she reached out with the handle of the umbrella and caught him around the neck.

"Don't break his neck, Mrs. Stirrup! Don't break

his neck!" Clotilde went on saying while Grandmother drew Pony Boy up to the edge where Harold
and Edmund could grab him.

"I have yet to break anyone's neck," said Grandmother.

When he was out on the bank gasping for breath
and spitting up canal water Grandmother asked
him, "What were you doing in the canal, young
man?"

"He was sailing leaf boats down to me on the
water," Theodora explained. "He was in his grove
and I was in ours."

"You were playing with Pony Boy?" I was
amazed.

"Oh, sure," my sister said. "We've been doing it
for a long time now. Demosthenes asked me one day
at school if I wanted to."

"Demosthenes!" Edmund and I said at once.

"Yes, that's his real name. He won't answer to it,
though."

"I would not wonder at that," said Grandmother.
She tilted her head to one side and looked critically
at Pony Boy, lying there in the dirt of our grove.
"Well, how are you? What do you have to say for
yourself, my boy?"

Pony Boy sat up now and coughed twice to get
the rest of the water out, all the time looking at

Grandmother. Then he opened his mouth and said a word.

"Thanks." Pony Boy had spoken.

We'd had our historic moment, to which Grandmother responded politely, "You are very welcome, young man."

Pony Boy and Anatola went home after that, but Harold and Clotilde stayed behind. They were saucer-eyed at Grandmother's daring. "Gosh, do all English people act like that—just like it was nothing at all—when they save somebody's life?" Harold wanted to know.

"Of course," said Edmund.

"Yes, every Englishman and Englishwoman knows his or her duty," Grandmother told them as she went back to her bench and her book. She picked up the novel she'd been reading. I saw it was *Ben Hur*. "We English are a Spartan lot. We never flinch," she remarked. She looked at the two remaining Appelbooms over the top of her spectacles. "My dears, how would you like to have me read the account of the chariot race to you? It is very exciting. Messala is a delightful villain."

"An American wrote that book—General Wallace," Harold told her, but he sat down at Grandmother's feet the way we all did.

"Some Americans do some things rather well,"

Grandmother answered him, "but I still feel that I can recommend Charles Dickens, an Englishman, to all of you."

Clotilde nudged me. "You come play with us next time in our grove, Amelia. I'll get Pa to let you keep bees if you want to."

Then we were quiet, to hear Grandmother.

That night after dinner I talked to Theodora in my room. I told her what Sung Lee had told Bill Lee about our "bad manners."

Theodora plunked herself down on my bed and scowled. "Oh, I hate that old Katherine Flanagan Thorup. It isn't fair the way she treats us. What are we going to do about that nasty old woman?"

"Something!" I told her. "The way I see it, she's one of the biggest flies in the Bromfield-Brown ointment. I'm going to see her—and I'm going Saturday." I made up my mind just then when I spoke. My decision was sudden, but I meant it.

"Oh," Theodora gasped.

"Do you want to come too?"

She put my pillow over her face. "No!"

"Well, then, I'm going alone. I won't ask Edmund. This is woman to woman. I'll have it out with her." I sounded braver than I felt. "But you and he can do something to help me out if I'm going to have to do all the dangerous work alone."

She came out from behind the pillow. "What, Amelia?"

"You play over in the Appelboom grove Saturday. I'll go over there with you, but I'll leave right away for the Thorups'. You and the Appelbooms will have to cover up for me."

Theodora's mouth was a round O. "All right, but what if Mother wants you, or Grandmother asks for you?"

"You'll have to think of something to tell them. And you won't be able to tell the Appelbooms where I'm going, either. I don't think I'll be gone very long, though."

"No?"

"No. She'll probably throw me out of the house right away."

"Oh, Amelia," Theodora wailed, "that would be terrible!"

I thought so, too, but just the same the next Saturday afternoon I pulled the bellpull at the door of the Thorup house. My knees were knocking together. I just hoped no one could see them shaking under my dress. I hadn't even been able to dress up to go calling, since I wanted to keep my going away from home a secret, but I did have my bonnet on. I'd thrown that out of my room the night before into the top of an orange tree, and Edmund had fetched

it for me. I hoped my pretty bonnet would be noticed and not my dress, which was a plain old blue
one.

Jennie opened the door. "Amelia!" she said. She
was surprised, but I was determined. I marched
right past her into the hall.

"I didn't come to see you or Robert today," I told
her. "I came to see your mother."

"Who is it, Jennifer?" I heard Mrs. Thorup call
from the parlor.

"It's Amelia, Mama."

"How nice!" Mrs. Thorup said, and she sounded
as if she meant it. "Have her come in here."

I straightened up as tall as I could get and stomped
into the parlor.

Mrs. Thorup had been playing cards with Jennie.
She picked them up and shuffled them when she
saw me. "Do you play whist, Amelia?" she asked me.
"You're about fourteen now, aren't you? That's old
enough to learn whist, I imagine."

"No." We didn't play card games in our house, we
read books, so I blurted out the name of the only
card game I knew—the game Mr. Mercer had mentioned. "I play poker."

Mrs. Thorup's eyebrows shot up a good half inch.
"My gracious!" she said.

I sat down without being invited. If she thought we

Bromfield-Browns had bad manners, let her go on thinking it. "I didn't come here to play cards," I told her.

She smiled and put the deck down on the table next to her. "Please tell Sung Lee to bring some milk and a piece of the currant cake for Amelia," she said to Jennie. When Jennie had gone to the kitchen she asked me, "Why did you come here, Amelia? There seems to be something on your mind."

I came right out with it. "I want to know what you meant when you said the Bromfield-Browns had bad manners. We don't have! Our manners are just as good as anyone else's and a lot better than most!"

She didn't even ask how I knew what she had said. Everyone took it for granted that servants talked a lot, particularly Chinese servants. "Well, Amelia, that *was* a rather strange invitation to tea we had from the Bromfield-Browns some months ago."

"I wrote that!" I flared.

"I know you did. Now tell me—would your mother have accepted an invitation written by Jennifer?"

I thought for a long moment, and I didn't enjoy what came out of my thoughts. "No, I don't think she would—but Uncle Hesketh and Jennie and Robert accepted mine!" I had Katherine Flanagan Thorup there.

"So you call him Uncle Hesketh?" She was smiling at me now. "What do you call me, I wonder?"

"Mrs. Thorup," I told her, but I didn't tell her that sometimes I called her other things in my mind, like "that awful woman," or "the fly in our ointment." "*He* came to our house to tea!"

"But, Amelia," she said in her gentle voice. "I have never had a proper invitation to tea. I scarcely know your family. Hesketh refuses to stand on ceremony. He has little use for the proprieties. He never has had."

I thought that must be true. After all, he had married her, and that had made him a remittance man.

"Would you come if my mother and my grandmother wrote an invitation to you?"

"Perhaps I would."

Just then Sung Lee came in with a tea tray, two glasses of milk, and a tall yellow cake dotted with purple currants. Jennie was right behind him.

"Ah, yes," she went on, when Jennie had sat down and Sung Lee, whose black eyes had bored holes into me with secret knowledge of why I was there, had gone back to the kitchen, "whatever happened in England is part of the past here in Riverside, Amelia. We are Americans now, and we Thorups are quite content here. We do not think about England anymore, and we do not dwell on what may have taken place there."

"Yes," said Jennie, "I don't even know the words to God *Save the Queen,* even though it has the same tune as *America.*" She looked at her mother. "What *did* happen in England, Mama?" Then Jennie gulped her milk, nearly as badly as Theodora did.

"Nothing at all of any importance, darling," Mrs. Thorup replied. She cut off a big slice of cake for me. "I know that Amelia understands what I mean. England is of no moment here, except for one thing —fundamental English manners!" She looked hard at me.

I knew what she meant, all right—"proper" invitations. Now it was up to me to see to it that Grandmother and Mother sent one to her. That wouldn't be easy, but at least I thought I'd learned a few things. I'd learned that Katherine Flanagan Thorup didn't hold the past against Grandmother. That would be helpful. I felt quite grown-up that she had treated me the way she did and trusted me to keep the secret from Jennie. Wild horses would never drag out of me that Hesketh Thorup was a remittance man. I thought it was pretty terrible that Uncle Hesketh *was* one. I would have welcomed his wife into our family in England.

It seemed to me that Katherine Flanagan Thorup

and Grandmother were out of the same mold. They ought to get along pretty well, once they knew one another. They were both so *English,* even if Mrs. Hesketh Thorup was Irish really. I sighed. How much simpler it would be if they had American manners, and were satisfied if people simply asked them to "drop in" sometime. They were stuffy, all right, but I guessed we'd have to live with that. They were too old to change much.

I was halfway home before I remembered I hadn't asked Mrs. Thorup to keep it a secret that I'd been to visit her. I had got sidetracked when I'd looked at the patterns for the new summer dresses she was going to make. They were beautiful. So was the gown she'd been wearing, green velvet with ball fringe like some of the draperies in Mr. Mercer's house. I was a little bit afraid as I went home. If my family ever found out, they would be furious. I'd gone behind their backs again.

I headed for the Appelboom place, hoping that Mother hadn't called for me or if she had, that Theodora had made up a believable story. I was getting more faith in Theodora all the time. She was becoming more and more like an American, and that seemed to make her independent and more grown-up. I hoped it wouldn't go to her head.

I turned in at the Appelbooms' front gate. Theodora jumped off the porch and ran down to meet me. "Did she throw you out into the street?" she asked me in a loud whisper.

"No," I said.

Theodora smelled of gooseberry preserves, which was what the Appelbooms liked best to eat, from what I'd seen of their school lunch pails.

"Our troubles are over—except for that horrible old white scale," I told my sister.

"What do you mean, Amelia?"

"The Tennis Club is in sight!"

I decided to put off asking Mother and Grandmother to send a "proper" invitation to Mrs. Thorup until Uncle Hesketh came home. Maybe I'd get Father in on it, too. They would want to see Hesketh when he came back from Australia anyway, and if Jennie, Robert, and he came to tea also, everything should work out all right. There was safety in numbers. I decided, too, I'd better tell Father and Mother what I'd done. I didn't think that they would be very angry with me, and I wasn't thrashed now that I was so grown-up.

I went to bed happy that night. I was so happy that I did something reckless. I took Mischief out of her basket and carried her upstairs with me, to let her sleep on my bed. I always slept with a window open, so she could stroll around on the roof if she wanted to, or she could go down the ivy vine to the ground.

It must have been about two o'clock in the morning when I woke up. I heard our clock strike twice, but I was too sleepy and too irritated to think about that much. Mischief was walking around on my chest. She was yowling and sneezing. I tried to push her away from me, but she kept on yowling. Then she sneezed again. Because she was making so much noise I really woke up. What if Grandmother and the others heard her, and knew that I had the cat upstairs? Grandmother and Mother didn't think Mischief should sleep with us, and Edmund and Theodora would be angry because I had the cat and they didn't. I put on my old blue wrapper and carpet slippers. Then I picked Mischief up and got out of bed. I'd have to take her back downstairs.

I opened my door; then I smelled something. It bit in my nose and I sneezed, too. My lamp on the table by the door was low, so I turned its button. Now I could see better. With Mischief under my arm and the lamp in my hand I went out into the hall.

The cat sneezed twice more as I went down the stairs. It was hard for me to get my breath somehow, yet I wanted to sneeze, too. What could it be?

Then I saw it—little pale curls of smoke drifting out from under the parlor door. I don't know why I did, but I put the cat down and grabbed the doorknob. It was so hot that it burned my hand. I let go of the knob in a hurry as Mischief scooted past me toward the kitchen.

Our parlor was on fire! Our house was on fire! I screamed, "Papa! Papa!" and ran to the landing, yelling.

They all started to come out of their bedrooms. Edmund was the first one on the landing with me. "What's the matter?" he asked.

"The house is on fire!"

Father was at the top of the stairs. Mother, Grandmother, and Theodora were behind him.

"The house is on fire, Papa!" Edmund yelled.

Father spoke quietly, first to my brother and sister. "You two go to the Appelbooms'. Wake them up. We may need help." He turned to Edmund. "Then take one of the grays, Edmund, and go for the firemen in Riverside."

As they fled down the steps, I called out to them over the railing, "The fire's in the parlor. Go out the kitchen door!"

Now Father spoke to me. "Amelia, get buckets from the shed. Bring water to the front door."

"I'll help Amelia," said Grandmother Thorup. She

was carrying her little canary bird in his cage. She'd only bought the bird that day. The cage bounced back and forth against the bannisters as she hurried out ahead of me toward the shed.

"What will Mother and Father do?" I gasped as I took a couple of buckets and went to the well. Grandmother had put down her birdcage and grabbed buckets, too.

"They'll put out the fire, Amelia!"

Then I saw Mother and Father stumble out of the house. Mother was holding the hem of her robe over her face and she was coughing. I guessed they'd stayed inside longer to check on the size of the fire. As I hurried onto the front porch with the first buckets I'd filled, I saw Edmund and Theodora running across the Queen's Own Grove to the Appelbooms'. In their nightclothes they looked like real ghosts this time, but it wasn't at all funny.

Father and Mother were at the front of the house by now. Mother was on the porch, but Father was inside in the hall. I gave the bucket to Mother, who passed it to Father. He threw it into the blaze through the open parlor door. The flames were high in there now. Then I gave Mother the other bucket to hand to Father. When both buckets were empty, I ran back to the well. Grandmother was already on the porch handing Mother one of her buckets. I tried to fill mine quickly, but it wasn't easy and the water-filled buckets were very heavy. I could hardly run with them.

I noticed on my third trip to the well that Edmund was carrying buckets now, too. "Why didn't you go get the fire fighters?" I shouted to him as we went past one another.

"Harold's going! It was his father's idea. Harold can ride bareback faster than I can. Mr. Appelboom's getting up and he'll be right over."

I only nodded and stumbled along to give my buckets to Mother and Father.

Father was outside on the porch now. "I think we're gaining on it," he told me. "There's only a little fire left. I couldn't get at it with the buckets from the doorway, but if I break the window I can."

So he took one of Grandmother's empty buckets and smashed in the parlor window in one great loud crash.

We learned afterwards from Mr. Appelboom that breaking the big bay window was the worst thing we could have done. We'd given the fire more oxygen. Flames blazed out of the window before Father could even put water on them from my buckets. The draperies caught fire at once and blew out onto the porch in tongues of flame. They singed Father's bathrobe, and he had to leap back for his life. I leaped, too, and then I threw my water at the flames, but my aim wasn't good and the water fell short onto the boards of the porch.

It was hopeless now. We'd let the fire have the air it needed to grow larger. We had to give up fighting it after I went for the next water buckets. It spread rapidly, and in a little while it had reached the upper story of the house. There was nothing we could do but stand in the Queen's Own Grove watching our home and everything in it burn down. At the end all we could see were roaring flames— then the rafters and the joists, nothing but the black skeleton of our house, silhouetted against the terrible eye-aching red of the fire.

All of the Appelbooms came to stand with us before the end came. Harold had gone to get the firemen, but now it was too late.

"We're sorry, folks," Mr. Appelboom said to us.

"We sure are," Mrs. Appelboom added.

Anatola saw Grandmother's canary bird, and it reminded her of something. "Where's the kitty cat? Where's Mischief?"

I had seen the cat, a black streak, heading for the canal minutes after I came outside. "She got out, Anatola. She's the one who woke me up."

"Maybe she saved our lives," said Edmund.

"That'd be nice," said Anatola.

Mr. Appelboom must have had very good ears. He

called out over the roaring of the flames as a rafter collapsed into the shell of our adobe lower story. "Hear the bells? The firemen are on their way."

"Too late," said Grandmother. Her voice was harsh. "I have ruined us all."

"You?" Father asked her.

"Yes, Roger. I neglected to blow out the kerosene lamp in the parlor tonight."

"But, Mother, I saw you blow it out. It must have been a spark from the fireplace," Mother protested.

"No, Enid. The fault is mine. I have not done a single thing correctly since we left London." A large tear rolled down her cheek.

Then the fire truck arrived, pulled by four white horses. It was large, and painted red and black and gold.

"You're too late." Mr. Appelboom did the talking to the men from Riverside. "The house's a goner."

Mrs. Appelboom was talking to Mother. "You poor dears," she said, "my spirits are sure low about this — just as low as yours are."

I didn't want her to go on talking about spirits, no matter what she meant, and I looked around for something to take her mind off them. Just then Mr. Mercer's carriage came rolling into our turnabout. "Look!" I called.

Grandmother took one look at the newcomer, let

out a little shriek, and fled behind an orange tree—one that hid her, but not the birdcage.

"What's *he* doing here?" I asked Clotilde.

"Oh, old man Mercer? He comes to all the fires in Riverside." Clotilde wasn't a bit perturbed, even if we were. She bit on one of her braids and then yawned.

Mr. Mercer got down from his carriage and came to stand with the firemen, watching as the last timber fell into the coals. Then he walked over to us and took off his hat, just as if we'd met him on Lemon Street or Magnolia Avenue. "I'm real sorry," he said to Father. "You people insured?" I could see his eyes roaming around, and I saw him spy the birdcage. How could he have missed it?

"Thank you, yes, Mr. Mercer, we're insured," Father told him.

"Not with Algie Somerset, I hope!" He sounded concerned.

Father could still laugh. "Thank heavens, no. We insured our property before we left London. We're insured with Lloyd's."

Mr. Mercer nodded. "It's all right, then. Lloyd's is a good firm. I heard of it. That'll take care of your goods that was in your house. But if you have to borrow money to build up the house again, you tell 'em at the bank that Mercer'll vouch for you." He took a cigar from his pocket. "Mind if I light up?" he asked Mother.

Mother laughed at that. I think she was a little bit hysterical. "Not at all," she said, and she gestured toward the mound of coals that had been our house. "Help yourself to a light."

"Where'll you be goin' now?" he wanted to know.

"The Glenwood Cottages, I suppose, for tonight, anyhow. We'll be looking for a house to rent tomorrow, to live in while we rebuild."

"No reason to do that—to look for a house, I mean," Mr. Mercer said to Father. "I got me a big empty house in my grove. I ain't gonna live in it again—not alone, I ain't." He glanced once more toward the orange tree and the birdcage. "You stay there while you do your rebuildin', and no rent, neither. I won't take no for an answer."

"Oh, we couldn't do—" Mother started to say. But Father stopped her with, "Thank you, Mr. Mercer. We accept with pleasure."

Mr. Mercer was happy to hear this. He grinned so widely that I saw half of his gold teeth. He certainly had a lot of them, too. Then he walked around the fire to my side and spoke more softly to me. "You can tell your grandma she can come out from behind that tree soon's I get away, little lady." He winked at me and bit the end of his cigar. "I saw her when I drove up. That pink's a purty shade on her. I like pink."

"The wrapper is white," I told him. "The fire makes it look pink."

"Purty," he repeated, as if he hadn't heard me at all. "I always did fancy pink. I like birds, too. My Minnie used to have 'em. In the summer they used to wake me up ever' morning at four a.m. with their singin' and throwin' birdseed around, but I never paid it much mind." He paused for a moment, then asked me, "Your grandma wasn't wearin' kid leather curlers, was she? My eyes aren't that good."

"Oh, no—she never does!" I breathed. I could tell that he hated kid curlers, and I was ashamed of mine. But then, Mr. Mercer didn't care how I looked. He wasn't interested in me.

He left after that, and so did everyone else, except Mr. Appelboom who went to get his wagon to drive us to the Glenwood Cottages in Riverside.

We stared solemnly at one another. "It's a good thing it wasn't blowing hard tonight," Father stated, "or we would have lost the carriage house and the sheds, too." He sighed. "We'll have to borrow money to build a new house, Enid."

"Yes, what we got for our oranges that we sent to market won't cover that," Mother agreed. As Grand-mother came out from behind her tree, Mother said,

"Well, I suppose that we *must* become Americans now. There's our last link with England—ashes, and what we have on our backs!"

There were tears in Mother's eyes and she put her head on Father's shoulder. I put my arms around Grandmother after Theodora took the birdcage. Edmund came back from the canal with Mischief under his arm.

"Well, there is one thing we can say." Father had the last word. "We're together, and we'll be all right. It isn't as if we haven't got friends, good friends, here in America."

Twelve   Vedalia Cardinalis

THE NEXT MORNING Mr. Appelboom came to the Glenwood Cottages bringing a suit of his own for Father and one of Mrs. Appelboom's dresses for Mother. They didn't fit very well, but at least our parents could go down into Riverside and Father could see the bankers, while Mother bought something for the rest of us to wear. We had a nice cottage, and the people at the hotel were kind to us, but we didn't want to go outside in our nightclothes.

That same afternoon we went to Mr. Mercer's wedding cake house, and my, how everyone's eyes popped when they saw it! I was glad Edmund and I had seen it first.

"Why, it's almost a palace!" Grandmother said. She was astonished. I think it was the first thing she had admired since we came to Riverside, except for Magnolia Avenue's pepper trees.

Father had the house key and in we went. The house was full of surprises. The dust sheets had been taken off the furniture, and, as we stood in the beautiful parlor, looking around at all the velvet and gilt paint, Bill Lee came in and bowed. We were surprised to see him there. In the confusion none of us had thought about him at all.

"Mr. Mercer, he come get me," Bill Lee explained. "He send wagonload groceries here, too. Stove going. Water run in kitchen pump. All in number one shape. Five relatives work here all morning to get place ready."

"This is a wonder, a real wonder!" Grandmother's voice floated back to us. She was going through the house, and now she called to Mother to follow her. "Oh, Enid, come see this painting."

"Old Missy Thorup, she going to marry Mr. Mercer?" Bill Lee asked Father.

Father was embarrassed. "I don't know, Lee."

"Bet Mr. Mercer does," said Edmund.

"Bet Grandmother doesn't know he wants to," said Theodora.

"Bet Grandmother does know it," I said.

Father changed the subject. "Well, Lee, are you sure you want to come back and work for us? We don't seem to be very lucky, do we? What with our house burning down."

Bill Lee was somber-faced. "I like Brown family," he said slowly. "They good to me. They Lee's family, too."

This made Edmund laugh and say, "Golly, Lee, that's silly. You don't need us. Just about everybody in Chinatown's a relation of yours."

But Bill Lee shook his head violently. "Not so, Mr. Edmund—not so. They be cousins, nephews, and brothers. All come from China, too, like me. All go back China someday to die. No family here, no children, only men and boys coming from China." He pointed to Theodora. "No see Chinese girl children—not ever! Law of United States not permitting Chinese men to bring brides from China."

Now I knew why I'd never seen any Chinese women or girls in Riverside. I felt sorry for Bill Lee.

"Oh, Lee, if you want us to, we'll be your family," said Theodora. She was crying.

"That what I want most of all. Come, see new kitchen." Theodora followed Bill Lee out, but at the door he stopped and spoke to Father and Edmund and me. "When Old Missy Thorup marry Mr.

Mercer, I go home with Brown family. I not stay here with Old Missy. Will send cousin of mine. Bill Lee go with family—not with house!"

Father didn't laugh, so neither did we.

"It'll be harder for Bill Lee to be an American than for us," said Edmund after a while. "Being English is closer to being an American than being Chinese."

"That is very true," said Father, who sat down and looked up at the ceiling of the fancy Mercer parlor.

Edmund sat down at Mr. Mercer's pianoforte and started to pick out a tune. For a while in England Grandmother had thought Edmund had musical inclinations, but she had been wrong. I went up-stairs for two reasons—to get away from Edmund and the piano, and to find Mother.

She was alone. Grandmother was taking a tour of the balcony that encircled three sides of the house. Mother was sitting on a huge bed, a bed with a scarlet satin cover and scarlet silk hangings. "This is a remarkable place," she told me with a little laugh. She sounded a bit hysterical again. "Good heavens, Mr. Mercer must be terribly rich. How will we ever go back to our own way of living after this?" She waved at the marble mantel and the gold-backed dresser set. Mr. Mercer's rooms had *everything* in them! I guessed he'd left his house just the way it was when his wife had died.

I sat down beside her. "Mother," I began, and then I stopped.

"Yes, Amelia, what is it?" Mother got up and went to the mirror to take off her bonnet.

"It's about Hesketh's wife. I went to see her."

"What?" Mother turned around, the bonnet still in her hand. "Why did you do that?"

So I told her the whole story as quickly as I could —about our "bad manners," my tea invitation, and about Mrs. Thorup's not hating Grandmother at all. "All's forgotten about England now," I finished, "and I think maybe all's forgiven, too."

Mother laughed again. "Well, Amelia, things do come thick and fast sometimes in America, don't they? I suppose I can prevail upon your grand-mother to send an invitation to Katherine Flanagan. That is what Katherine wants, I suspect, not an in-vitation from me." She sat down and looked into the mirror at me, behind her. Her face was sterner now. "Please don't do that sort of thing anymore, though, Amelia! It's dangerous. Your father and Hesketh are friends. You could have ruined that—or if not ruined it, you could have made it difficult for them."

She was right. I had taken a terrible chance.

Mother went on, "It isn't really our place to send

the first invitation, you know, not when *we* are the newcomers."

I said what I thought now. "It was Grandmother who was rude to *her* in England. I think Mrs. Thorup might be afraid Grandmother would be rude again over here. She'd come, though, if she got invited. Why don't you just ask all of the Thorups when Uncle Hesketh gets home, and not tell Grandmother?"

"No." Mother was firm. "Absolutely not. That would not be fair to your grandmother. She must know about it."

"All right. It was just an idea."

"How many other ideas have you had, Amelia?" Mother asked me.

"None, really. All I've tried to do is to get Grandmother into the Tennis Club."

"It's not the Tennis Club I'm thinking of," said Mother. "It's the people who live next door."

"What people?" I saw my face in the mirror and I tried to look innocent.

"The Appelbooms, Amelia."

"Oh, them. What about them?"

"They became friendly so *quickly*. Did you have something to do with that? Mrs. Appelboom says the strangest things to me sometimes."

I didn't lie to Mother. Halloween was long past, anyway. "It was Bill Lee's idea. We helped out his relation, Wing Lee, and we did a good thing. If I tell you, you'll have to promise me that you'll never say anything to anybody about it."

"I promise."

I told her of the Halloween séance and why we did it.

This time Mother giggled. She put her handkerchief up to her mouth while her shoulders shook. "Oh, dear, Amelia," she said finally. "I'll keep your secret, but do let me tell your father."

"You aren't angry with us?"

"No, no, not angry—but it was dangerous. Please give up Halloween pranks. They aren't ladylike."

I didn't promise that. I figured I had one more year of being wicked ahead of me before I was too grown-up. Besides, I hadn't been in America long and hadn't known how much fun Halloween could be. "Does Mrs. Appelboom suspect what I did?" I asked.

"No, dear, she doesn't. But I know now what she means when she asks me if we have spirits in our house, too."

I had to laugh. "Oh—she means ghosts, and things from 'the beyond.' " In England *spirits* meant brandy and whisky, but Americans called such things *liquor*.

Mother stopped laughing now. "Yes, I never could understand what she meant. At first I thought she was a member of the Women's Christian Temperance Union, trying to learn if we had alcoholic beverages in our house. After a time, though, I thought I'd better offer her a glass of port or sherry. I did that once, but she refused it. She seemed a bit shocked by it, too, I might add."

Just then Mother put her finger to her lips. She needn't have. I'd heard Grandmother's footsteps coming along the balcony, too.

My talk with Mother was over. I never thought when I went up to find her that I'd end up telling everything I knew. It made me sigh. I guessed I wasn't quite as grown-up as I'd thought I was, even though I was going to go into the high-school class in September.

Grandmother simply couldn't get over how fine Mr. Mercer's house was. She had a wonderful bedroom—one with a huge golden oak wardrobe and a bed fit for Queen Victoria herself, she said. Her room was purple and gold, which made her feel very regal.

I saw Mr. Mercer in his grove quite often after school. His oranges ripened later than ours had, and he came to supervise the picking and the packing. I watched him and his workers use the Bromfield-Brown water method on his oranges. I waved when he waved to me, but he never came to the house. I wished that Grandmother would ask him to tea, but she didn't, and I kept my promise to Mother not to put out any more surprise and "improper" invitations to grown-ups.

It was all right to invite the Appelboom kids, though, and they came to see the Mercer house right off. So did Jennie and Robert, who were friends now with the Appelbooms, too. We liked our American friends and wanted to be like them most of the time. I really wasn't too sorry that we'd lost our English clothes in the fire. Now we dressed like Riversiders, like Americans.

Robert said we were even losing our English accents, but we couldn't see that until Grandmother confirmed it by saying at supper that the way Edmund was speaking, she couldn't tell him from Dunstan Appelboom.

"You can sure tell him from Pony Boy, though, can't you, Grandmother?" Theodora said.

"Oh, I can, indeed!" Grandmother said, laughing. She was mellowing all right.

Hesketh Thorup came home the last day of April. But we didn't see him, for he only stayed one day in Riverside, and then off he went again—this time to Washington, in the District of Columbia.

Robert told us about it at school. "He has to see somebody in Washington," was all he would say, but we could tell by the way he acted that he knew something. Robert was very excited.

"He'll be back pretty soon," Jennie confided to me.

We could hardly wait, but that's what we had to do. Everyone in town wondered what Uncle Hesketh had found out in Australia. I even asked Mr. Mercer about it a few days after Hesketh had gone away again. "Did Uncle Hesketh talk to you when he was here?"

"No, little lady, he didn't. He wasn't in town long enough to do more than take a look around to see if Riverside's still here. Guess he found out it was, and off he went again, huh?"

"Yes, sir." I was disappointed.

"How's your grandma like my house?"

"She thinks it's a palace. Grandmother likes palaces. We think she used to pretend she was Queen Victoria. But I don't believe she does that anymore."

Mr. Mercer laughed. "Maybe, then, you might tell her my first name's Albert. Most folks calls me Bert, though—my name sure ain't Prince Albert."

Even Americans knew that Prince Albert had been Queen Victoria's husband.

"Oh, I'll tell Grandmother," I said. It might make

a difference, I thought. She might like him better when she knew his name was Albert.

"Think your grandma might like to go buggy ridin' with me someday? I got me a new mare, half Arab. She cost me a pretty penny, let me tell you. She's quite a stepper. Her name's Zuleika. Your grandma likes horseflesh, don't she?"

"Oh, yes," I told him. It was true. Grandmother liked horses better than she liked most people.

Then he went off to talk to his foreman about cutting down some trees that weren't bearing well.

I told Grandmother what Mr. Mercer had said about buggy riding and Zuleika, and that his first name was Albert. She just nodded and went right on reading *Uncle Tom's Cabin,* the American book that the librarian had recommended to her.

"Will you go buggy riding?" I asked her.

"I shall consider it, Amelia," she replied. "The next time you see Mr. Albert Mercer, you may tell him that I send my cordial regards to him and thank him for the hospitality of his house."

"I don't think that's going to satisfy him," I said under my breath.

"What was that, child?" She looked up at me.

"I said, 'I'll tell him.' "

Hesketh came back again the end of May. A fruit

growers' meeting was called for the second night he was home. We were very excited about the meeting. We hoped there'd be good news about white scale from the international exposition at Melbourne. I begged so hard to go that Father finally gave in, saying that if I fell asleep he'd leave me there in the Grand Army of the Republic lodge hall.

Theodora and Edmund wanted to go, too, but Father told them that the meeting would be long and dull.

I finally said to Theodora, "Look at the way you went to sleep the night of the killer frost. This is important, too—maybe."

"I hope it will be." Mother wasn't so sure.

"I hope it *won't* be," said my disagreeable brother, who couldn't go.

The G.A.R. hall was almost full when we arrived, but there were some seats in the front row. It was embarrassing to go down there with everybody watching, but we had to do it all the same. I was glad that I was wearing my yellow taffeta dress and my new bonnet with the white flowers and white ribbon ties.

Mr. Mercer and Uncle Hesketh were on the platform. They both smiled at me. That made me feel better. I looked around, but I didn't see anyone else my age. Jennie and Robert weren't there, either.

Uncle Hesketh looked a little tired. He must have been thirsty, too, because he poured a drink of water from a pitcher. Then he took three little glass bottles out of his vest pockets and put them on the table in front of him.

"You all know the many things we have attempted here in Riverside to stamp out white scale," he said. "We've tried washes of every sort. Some of us have fumigated our groves and killed our trees. Nothing has been successful." He paused for breath and went on. "Orange trees in Australia are also afflicted with white scale but, as you know, it does not spread in that country. As a matter of fact, it seems to be dying out. I spoke to scientists and citrus growers in Melbourne. They believe that they know what controls white scale."

It was so quiet in the G.A.R. hall now that I was convinced no one present in the audience was even breathing.

"Yes, they were very kind to me in Melbourne and most helpful, too. They did not send me back empty-handed." He pointed to the three little bottles. "What you are now going to see may mean the end of white scale in southern California forever!" He came to the edge of the platform and, to my astonishment, looked down at me. "Come up here, please, Amelia."

I was so surprised that I couldn't budge from my chair. I didn't move until Father said, "Go on up, Amelia. Everyone is staring at us."

"But everyone'll be looking at me if I go up there!"

"Go up, Hesketh wants you to," Father said.

I got up and went slowly up the platform. I felt that thousands of people were watching me, but there were only about a hundred or so. Just the same I was afraid.

Hesketh gave me the first bottle. "What's in it, Amelia?" he asked me. "Tell the ladies and gentlemen."

I looked into the bottle. All I could see was a dead insect. I didn't know what kind it was.

"A dead insect," I called out.

He smiled and gave me bottle number two. "What is this?"

"Another dead insect," I said loudly, feeling silly. I hadn't ever seen this one before, either—at least, I didn't think I had.

"And this." He handed me the third bottle with a real flourish.

I looked at it, too. It had *three* dead insects in it. They were red with black spots, and they had little wings. I knew what they were. I'd seen them in our rose garden in England. "They're three ladybird beetles—but they're dead, too." I was disappointed.

"They are called ladybugs here"—everyone laughed when Uncle Hesketh said this—"but if Amelia had noticed the label on the bottle, she would have seen that it reads *Vedalia cardinalis*. That is the scientific name for these insects." He smiled at me. "Thank you, Amelia. You may sit down now."

I went back to my seat. I knew that I was blushing. My knees were trembling, so I took my bonnet off and put it over them, but it wasn't heavy enough to hold them down so I put it on again.

Hesketh went on talking. "One, perhaps two, or maybe all three of these insects eat white scale in both the larval and adult stages. They say in Melbourne that by 1890 we should be able to wipe out white scale in our groves completely—if one condition is met!"

"What's the condition?" a grower stood up and yelled out.

Hesketh answered him. "That the insects survive here in this country and multiply. In Melbourne they predicted that they would."

Someone in the hall started to cheer; then so did everybody else. In a moment Mr. Mercer stood and held up his hands for quiet. Finally he had to outshout the audience, and it wasn't easy for him even though he did have a loud voice.

After a while Hesketh got to speak again. "I've

been to Washington and I've talked to men in the Department of Agriculture. They say we can import these useful insects. Shall we send to Australia for them?"

"Yes!" shouted Mr. Appelboom, who was sitting in the row behind us.

Uncle Hesketh was finished. He sat down while everybody clapped and stamped their feet so hard that I thought the walls of the G.A.R. hall would cave in.

Now Mr. Mercer got up again. "I say we give three cheers to Mr. Hesketh Thorup, a good friend to Riverside and to all of us."

The crowd cheered, "Hurrah! Hurrah! Hurrah!"

"Now there's somebody else here deservin' thanks," Mr. Mercer continued. "He's the man who figured out how to tell good oranges from frozen ones! You come on up here, Mr. Brown."

Father turned pink and stayed in his chair. "Go up, Papa," I told him in his own words, "Mr. Mercer wants you to."

Father rose and went up on the platform, and stood with Hesketh and Mr. Mercer.

Mr. Mercer bellowed out, "We got a lot to thank two Englishmen for here in Riverside. I think they're turnin' out to be pretty good Americans, don't you?"

Father got cheered three times, too. I was so

proud I thought I would burst. I was sorry that I had forgotten to bring a handkerchief, but Mrs. Appelboom reached over my shoulder and gave me hers. While I wiped my eyes all of the men in the hall came up to the platform and milled around, looking at the bottles of insects and shaking hands with Uncle Hesketh and Father.

It was a wonderful, wonderful night—the best we'd had since we came to Riverside. It was the best I'd ever had!

Uncle Hesketh came home with us and had a glass of brandy with Mother and Grandmother. Grandmother seemed very happy to see him and talked to him a lot. Father had invited Mr. Mercer, too, but he wouldn't come. I knew he'd come only if Grandmother asked him.

Grown-ups made me sigh with exasperation sometimes. Everything could have come right that night if only Mr. Mercer hadn't been so stubborn, and if Katherine Flanagan Thorup hadn't had a headache and stayed away from the fruit growers' meeting. We could have got them all together at our house. Mrs. Hesketh Thorup had picked a very bad time to have a headache, and Mr. Mercer needn't have been so silly. He didn't use very good grammar most of the time, but his manners were just as fussy as Grandmother's.

I got five minutes alone with Uncle Hesketh in

the kitchen. He came out to say hello to Bill Lee, which I thought was very nice of him. Bill Lee understood, as he always did, when I came out, too. He let me get Hesketh into a corner alone.

My, but I talked fast! I knew that I didn't have much time before Mother would come out after us. I told him about Grandmother and how unhappy she was in Riverside. I told him she blamed herself for our house burning down, when it hadn't been her fault at all. Then I told him that I'd gone to see his wife.

"I know that part of it, Amelia," he said. "That was all right. Kate likes you. She says you've got spunk. She'd like to come here to tea."

"We'll invite you all now that *you're* back," I said honestly, "but maybe Grandmother won't like it. It's really your wife's place to ask us first."

He touched his mustache. "That's true, Amelia, very true, you know."

"Well, there's one way around it," I went on breathlessly with my eye on the door.

"What would that be, now?"

"The Tennis Club! Please, can you get your wife to ask Grandmother to the Tennis Club to tea?"

"Ah yes, the Tennis Club. That would be neutral ground, wouldn't it?" He nodded his head. "Yes, Amelia, I will try to arrange it."

I wanted to kiss him, so I did. He didn't seem to mind it. "Oh, it's all so wonderful!" I exploded.

Uncle Hesketh smiled at me and shook his head a little. "You may not think so, Amelia, if I can arrange an invitation. My wife will probably think it best to send an invitation to the three of you."

"Father and Mother, too, you mean?"

"No. Your grandmother, your mother, and you."

"Me—why me?"

The corner of his mouth twitched a little. "I am careful of your father's health, Amelia, although he assures me that he is all right now. But the Tennis Club is something of an ordeal. I have noticed that women survive its rigors best."

Two days after that it came—an invitation to tea at the Casa Blanca Tennis Club, written by Mrs. Hesketh Thorup.

Grandmother pretended not to care particularly, but she was really in seventh heaven. What should she wear to such a place? What would Mother wear? What would I wear?

"Something simple, I believe," Mother said, when Grandmother took her new dove-gray silk dress out of the wardrobe. That was one thing about a fire. It did give a person a lot of new things to wear.

"Yes, Enid, it could be warm, couldn't it?" Grandmother commented.

I had to giggle. It was as hot as the dickens already, and it was only May, but Grandmother barely seemed to notice it now. She said she thought that she was becoming "acclimated" to Riverside's weather. I didn't think that I'd ever be. Girls in petticoats were at a disadvantage in hot climates.

The great day finally arrived. We all left promptly at three-thirty, dressed in our "simple" white muslin dresses and white Milan braid bonnets. Grandmother's bonnet had purple violets on it, Mother's had pink carnations, and mine had a wreath of yellow daisies around its crown to match my yellow silk sash. We smelled of violet water and Florida water. I had my hair up, and my Paris bangs, my new hairstyle, were right today at last. My skirts were long, but more than that I was wearing a corset for the first time, a Patent Roman corset. After I put it on, I knew that the Tennis Club was going to be a trial—and not for whatever reasons Uncle Hesketh had in mind. I had never been so grown-up before, or so uncomfortable, either. There was something to be said for childhood, I decided, but I didn't tell Mother that.

We Bromfield-Browns hadn't been so fashionable since we'd been driven about London by Cook's husband to see our English relations. Grandmother drove our grays, and as we went down Magnolia

Avenue she nodded to the left and to the right, just as she'd done in our carriage in England. She was happy now. I thought she looked much more like "the dashing Mrs. Stirrup" than she did like Queen Victoria.

The Casa Blanca Tennis Club was only a little wooden house on Adams Street. There were tennis courts near it, so I supposed people did play tennis there, but the only people I saw sat on chairs on the porch of the Club and on its steps and drank tea. I learned afterwards that the Club gave balls and card parties in other places which were bigger, but I didn't think too much of the famous Tennis Club myself.

Katherine Flanagan Thorup was very pleasant to Mother and Grandmother, and we sat with her and her group of Riverside ladies. It was a real ordeal, drinking tea and saying, "No, thank you, I don't care for lemon," and "Thank you, I like sugar," and "Yes, I would like another petit four," for a whole long hour. I was on my very best behavior for several reasons—to please Mother, to put our best foot forward for Grandmother's sake, and because I was the only one of my age there. They were mostly ladies older than my mother, but they all fussed over me and said I was "a dear" and "charming" and I tried to like it. But it was so hot that my feet had swelled in my new shoes, and they hurt. I felt like the little mermaid in the fairy tale, and now I knew what Mother had meant when she said that "it hurts to be beautiful!"

Everyone talked about "useful insects" and Uncle Hesketh's trip to Australia. It was easy to tell which members of the Tennis Club were from England and which weren't. The Americans all called ladybirds "ladybugs." I decided that's what I would call them, too. I guessed we'd be hearing a lot about ladybugs from now on.

Grandmother wheezed a great deal from happiness. She didn't even bristle when people called Mother "Mrs. Brown." I thought she'd be very angry when a lady called her "Mrs. Stirrup," but she corrected her gently and said that her name was Thorup, too.

"Oh, then you and Hesketh are related?" that lady asked.

"Indeed we are!" Grandmother replied proudly, to my amazement. I hadn't thought she'd go that far.

Katherine Flanagan Thorup surprised me even more when she added, "Yes, Mrs. Thorup's husband was Hesketh's uncle—his very favorite uncle!"

"Yes," said Grandmother. She didn't try to add anything more to that. Mother and I were looking

down into our teacups. She told me afterwards that
Mrs. Thorup's remark was known as a "social white
lie."

After the hour was up, we took our leave, and we
were asked to come back again any time we chose.
That meant we were in the Tennis Club!

"My," said Grandmother as we turned off Adams
Street, "that was an enjoyable afternoon, wasn't
it?"

My Patent Roman corset was making me melt inside my clothes. "I'm glad you thought so," I told
her. "I don't want to go again. I'm so full of tea I'm
sloshing around inside."

"You won't have to go again, Amelia. You behaved most properly, and I was proud of you." I had
been praised by Grandmother! I was so astonished
that I kept quiet for a whole quarter mile.

We were on Magnolia Avenue now, going back to
the Mercer house. In spite of my shoes and corset I
was happy. White scale would be licked—I knew it
in my bones. We were friends with the Appelbooms,
and by September we'd be back home in our new
house in the Queen's Own Grove. Grandmother was
in the Tennis Club. What more could we want? I
asked myself. I loved America. I loved California. I
loved Riverside.

There was only one "ointment fly" left, and it

wasn't a big one. That ointment was one I was going to keep out of, though.

We saw another carriage coming toward us. It was Mr. Mercer out on his usual rounds, going from his alfalfa ranch to his grove. This time he had his new horse in the shafts, a little black one with the shiniest hide I'd ever seen. Zuleika was a beauty, just as he had said.

He spied us, of course, and whipped off his hat to bob his head three times, once to each of us. He grinned, too, but only at Grandmother.

She inclined her head to him and gave him a tiny smile. When he had passed us, she nudged me with her elbow. "Amelia," she said.

"Yes, Grandmother?"

"The next time you see Mr. Mercer, you tell him that he may call."

I was an American by now, I guessed, but I wasn't sure that Grandmother would ever be one. Why hadn't she just reined in the grays and asked him to Sunday supper? That would have been the simple thing to do. That's what anybody else would have done. That's what I would have done.

I sighed. "I think you'd better send Mr. Mercer an invitation."

That was all I had to say—that was all I would ever have to say. I was done with giving invitations out. Not me—not Amelia Brown!

Author's Notes

Late in the last century many Englishmen came to the Riverside area with their families to recover from tuberculosis. The trans-Canada pattern of the Bromfield-Browns was the common one; the English left the British Empire reluctantly. There were "remittance men," too, in and around Riverside in its early days, but, like Hesketh Thorup, they were far from being Wild West desperate characters.

Today, as then, Riverside is famed for its fine oranges. The struggle against white scale, known to scientists and entomologists as "cottony-cushion scale," actually took place. In 1887 the orange groves faced extinction, but by 1890 they had been saved by *Vedalia cardinalis,* the ladybug. In *The*

Queen's Own Grove Hesketh Thorup goes to Australia in search of something to control the pest. The actual historic savior and traveler was Albert Koebele. I have dramatized the introduction of the "useful insect" to the fruit growers for the purposes of the novel. The story of the discovery of a method of telling frozen oranges from edible ones is also based on fact. Credit for this finding should really be given to E.A. Chase.

The stores, hotels, and streets mentioned in *The Queen's Own Grove* actually existed in the Riverside of 1887, though all the characters in the book are fictional. The Casa Blanca Tennis Club is part of history, too, and was the goal of the socially minded newcomers to the area in the 1880's. The stuffy Victorian manners of some of my characters were also factual. I would like to believe that southern California tempered these manners somewhat, but I am doubtful that it did.

The background material for *The Queen's Own Grove* came from a good many sources. I used John Brown and James Boyd's *San Bernardino and Riverside Counties,* of course, and Thomas Patterson's recent book, *Landmarks of Riverside,* which is replete with old photographs. Also very useful were issues of *The Riverside Daily Press* of 1887 and 1888.

Certain people were particularly helpful to me in my research. They gave of their time, advice, and reminiscences. I wish particularly to thank Dr. Ralph March and Dr. Leo Klotz of the world-famed Citrus Experiment Station of the University of California at Riverside for answers to questions about orange growing in the early days and about biological control. My gratitude is also expressed to Gabrielle Waugh, Esther Klotz, Phyllis Dole, Ethelbert Dole and his family, and to Thomas Patterson of the *Riverside Press Enterprise* for their interest and enthusiasm.

PATRICIA BEATTY

RIVERSIDE, CALIFORNIA

JANUARY, 1965

Patricia Beatty was born in Oregon in 1922 and graduated from Reed College in Portland. She resided in Riverside, California, for many years, before her death in 1991. She had a gift for writing historical fiction with characters infused with lively humor and drama. She won many honors including the Jane Adams award in 1972 for "Lupita Manana" about a brother and sister fleeing from the poverty of Mexico to Riverside County and the Scott O'Dell award for "Charley Skeddadle" in 1988 about a 12 year old drummer boy caught up in the Civil War. "Turn Homeward Hannalee," "Be Ever Hopeful Hannalee," "Eight Mules From Monterey," "Jayhawker," "The Nickel-Plated Beauty," "Sarah & Me & The Lady From the Sea,"Wait for Me Watch for Me Eula Bee," and "The Coach That Never Came" remain in print.

Patricia Beatty and her first husband John Beatty established an annual award for a children's book written with an authentic California background. At the time of her death at age 69, she left a husband, Carl Uhr, daughter Ann Alexandra and two grandchildren.